Tethered Angel

Struggles of the Women Folk Part 2

ဆာ

By T.M. Brown

To Lillian,

Enjoy !

T. M. Brown

Feb. 2018

Cover design by CC Morgan Design Visuals
Photo by Melissa Brown
Editing by Karen Perkins, LionheART Publishing House

More Books by T. M. Brown

A Life Not My Own

Struggles of the Women Folk

The short story, *TINAAH* is available in the anthology,
Just Between Us – Inspiring Stories by Women

To anyone out there who has struggled to find her place in the world. Know that you are not alone. There is light at the end of the tunnel, but you must continue moving forward.

Tethered Angel is the story of Georgie's daughter, Angel, who allows herself to be abducted by Miss Emily Barker. Angel was not taken by force but rather succumbed to Miss Emily Barker's promises of an extravagant life, lavishly traveling around the world. Follow them as they travel throughout Europe, meeting interesting people who will forever change Angel's life.

Will Angel ever return home? Will her mother, Georgie, ever see her again? Will Miss Emily Barker's wealth solve all of her problems?

Into The World

We spoke to one another about the world that Momma lived in from our small, dark place, not with words, but with feelings that were as natural as the nourishment that Momma gave us. We found comfort in wrapping our arms and legs around each other, floating in our Momma's love. I loved the sound of his steady heartbeat and would fall asleep in the comfort of it. He called himself my big brother, not because he was older than me, but because he was so much bigger than me. That was true even in the small space that was our perfect home. He begged me to be the first to enter this world, knowing that he would only be in it for a split second.

You have to go first. This world is not ready for me yet. There's no place in it for a black male child to prosper. People will be more accepting of you. You won't be as intimidating to them, because you are a girl. And Momma will raise you proper. There will be challenges ahead, but know that you are well prepared. And that I will never be too far from you, he said.

So when Aunt Adele told Momma to push, I was the first to leave. Charlie (that's what Momma and Aunt Adele named him) and I were holding hands until the very last minute. *I'll see you again, I promise,* he said as the light of the world blinded me upon entering it.

Charlie was already gone before Aunt Adele finished cleaning me up. Lifelessly, Charlie lay there in the pulled-out dresser drawer beside me. Already gone even before Momma or Aunt Adele realized it. I prayed that I would remember all the things we shared in our safe place. For our conversations would have to last me a lifetime—or at least this one.

*

It was a day just like any other day. Momma had forced me to take a nap on that hot summer's day. But that didn't matter to me. I still kept the covers pulled up tightly around my neck so that the spirits could not touch me. They'd come up real close to my face and talk to me, especially during my dreams. Sometimes they would tell me about things that were going on in our town and sometimes they would warn me about something that was about to happen to Momma. That's how I knew about the man who had hurt Sissy long ago. *The last one gone now. Tell Georgie, she safe now*, Sissy said as she stood beside my bed, appearing to be no more than a shadow that scared me to death. Just like Charlie, Sissy didn't speak out loud but talked to me with her intensely piercing eyes. I could hear her words as clearly as if they were spoken. She talked to my mind with her eyes. I guess it's true what they say about the eyes being the passageway to the soul. I just wish they would leave me alone.

When I told Momma what Sissy said, she pretended that she wasn't moved by it, but Momma didn't know that I could hear her thoughts. *Glad that bastard's gone. I hope all of 'em rot in hell*, was what Momma thought when my message to her came true. She tried to explain to me as best she could that what I had was a gift. Well, it sure didn't feel like a gift. Maybe Momma thought so, because I didn't tell her everything that I could see or how badly the kids at school treated me because of my so-called gift of second sight. Calling me a witch or worse.

"My momma say you got that second sight cuz you a bastard child. You ain't got no daddy. He lives on the other side of town. Your momma so poor, your daddy rather be with dat big ole, fat lady, Sally. My momma say yo momma a whore and dat gift you got came from the devil. She say I ain't supposed to talk to you," said one of the girls in my class as all the other children pointed and laughed at me. Those kids were so mean to me. Every day, I ate my lunch by myself and every day I lied to Momma when I returned home to her questions about how my day was. I couldn't wait for summer to start.

Momma would spend the summer working for Miss Emily Barker in the big house. She forced me to come along and made me "stay out of the way". I must have heard Momma tell me that at least ten times every day. Each time she said it, Miss Emily Barker would invite me to "keep her company". In no time, I was spending all my days with Miss Emily Barker, while Momma worked in her kitchen down in the basement with Ricky the cook.

"You ready to be happy now, Momma?" I asked her after seeing her and Ricky getting married in one of my dreams. I knew it wasn't going to last. Momma was so lonely and too easily taken advantage of because of it.

Miss Emily Barker thought she was fooling me too but I could read her mind like an open book. Didn't need to have second sight for that! "You gonna stick with our plan," she whispered to Ricky as he brought our tea on the front porch while Momma was downstairs sweating to death in the hot kitchen.

"I think we need to talk about this some more. She ain't nothing like you said she was."

"That's because you don't want to see it. But you see this sweet child, don't you? She deserves better."

"Now that . . . I can't deny."

"Then we need to stick to our plan," Miss Emily Barker insisted.

"What plan?" I interrupted, pretending not to know what they were talking about.

"Never you mind! This is grown folks talking," snapped Miss Emily Barker.

"Oh, I'm sorry, sweetie," she said, quickly composing herself. "It's just so hot that it's got me agitated! I can't wait until we leave this place and go to Europe where the weather is more agreeable. You gonna love it there, sweetie. Isn't that right, Ricky?" she asked as Ricky quickly exited the front porch without responding.

I should have told Momma right then and there what they were planning. But I wanted to go to Europe. I didn't want to leave Momma but I wanted to see all the beautiful places Miss Emily Barker had been telling me about. I wanted all of it because living here was just too hard for me. Miss Emily Barker promised to buy me dresses from Paris, take me to see the castles in Germany, and introduce me to lots of kids my age who would accept me. Kids who wouldn't tease me. Miss Emily Barker said the kids here were just jealous because they weren't as smart as I was. I knew that she was mostly lying but I just wanted to leave this place. I had to believe that there was somewhere better than this where I would fit in.

I just couldn't stand it any longer. The kids at school made fun of me all the time. Yes, we were poor. There was no denying that. Most of the kids at school lived in houses with running water and toilets and here we were, still stumbling our way to the outhouse in the middle of the night, even in the dead of winter. I never said anything to Momma because I knew that she was doing the best she could. But I wanted more. Silly as it sounds, I wanted indoor plumbing!

Miss Emily Barker talked to me intelligently and treated me like I was just as smart as she was. Momma treated me like a child, smothering me with lots of hugs and kisses. I knew Momma loved me, but it was just too much. It was the wrong kind of love. If only she had a man to give some of that attention to. She didn't know that I heard her crying in the night way too often. For years, she prayed to the Lord to send her a man to love her. She'd only known one man, just one time: my daddy. Even at a young age, I understood how lonely Momma was. I felt her pain and it hurt me as well.

So I played along with Miss Emily Barker's plan and justified it all by believing that Momma would be happy, if only for a short time. And she was, I could see that Ricky cared for her but he too had gotten himself caught up in Miss Emily Barker's scheming ways. Momma could have seen it too, if she could only believe in herself enough to see the world as it truly was instead of how she wanted it to be.

"I don't trust that white woman now further than I can throw her," Momma would say when she thought I wasn't listening. And she was right.

Every time Momma's back was turned, Miss Emily Barker would tell me that I deserved a better life. "What did you have for dinner last night?" she'd ask me. "If you were my child, we'd have four-course meals every night. You'd have servants waiting on you hand

and foot. You'd wear the finest clothes from Paris, France. You and I would travel all over the world."

I wanted all those things but I didn't want to leave my momma. "Is my momma coming with us?" I'd ask.

"No, I'm afraid not, dear. I asked her to come along with us. She said she has to take care of a few things here and maybe she will meet us later. But she loves you, Angel, and only wants what's best for you as do I, dear." I hated it when she called me dear because it was a sure indication that whatever she said before using that word was a lie. "Your momma wants you to go with me, dear. She just doesn't want you to think that she doesn't love you, dear." These were the lies that came out of her mouth. *No way I'm gonna take that backwards talking, country-assed mammy with us.* These were the words she thought.

"Please don't say anything to your momma about our plans. It will only make it more difficult for her to let you go. She might even make you stay until she's ready to leave. You want to go with me don't you, Angel? We'll tell her right before we leave. There's no need to have her upset for weeks, dear," whispered Miss Emily Barker during the wedding rehearsal for Momma and Ricky.

Momma was all caught up in having a husband and finally feeling like a respectable woman. She allowed herself to believe that Ricky loved her. It didn't take much to fool her. Ricky was nice to Momma but he was also nice to Miss Emily Barker.

"Sshh! She ain't gonna catch us. She's downstairs cooking," said Miss Emily Barker seductively as she pulled Ricky by his belt buckle into her bedroom, right next to the room that I was supposedly napping in. "I don't know how much more of this I can take, watching you pretend to love her. You belong to me. We belong together," she whispered in between the kisses while slowly unbuttoning his pants.

"Emily stop! This ain't gonna work if you keep sneaking kisses. You'll ruin everything . . ." Ricky said. *This woman done lost her mind. She think she own me!* he thought as he pulled away from her, tucked his shirt back into his pants and returned downstairs to the basement kitchen with Momma. *Don't nobody own me!*

Gone

Ricky and Momma were married in Miss Emily Barker's front yard just as she planned. That night while they honeymooned at Momma's house, we changed into the traveling clothes that Miss Emily Barker had hidden away for us and prepared to leave.

"Angel, do you have your letter? Good dear." Miss Emily Barker grimaced; proud of the plot that she was placing in motion.

We folded all of my old clothes neatly into two piles on her bed with a letter on each pile. One from Miss Emily Barker and one from me. My letter was full of apologies. I never saw what Miss Emily Barker's letter said.

"Well, I guess it's time for us to leave now, dear," she said, fastening the last button on my crisp white blouse that matched my gray knee-length skirt with thin white pinstripes. I was twelve years old and unlike Momma, Miss Emily Barker dressed me like a young lady and not a little child the way Momma always did. I could hardly recognize myself as I stood in front of the full length mirror in Miss Emily Barker's bedroom. I couldn't help but smile as I smoothed out my skirt stripes to perfection. This was the life I wanted.

After closing the last of the eight suitcases and placing them at the top of the stairs, Miss Emily Barker called for the driver, Mr. Paul, to place them in the shiny black car she rented to take us the ferry boat. She made sure to hire a driver from two towns over who didn't know anyone in our town. She had it all planned out so perfectly.

I'd never been in a car before. Momma and I walked anywhere that we needed to go. The white folk would speed by us in their shiny new cars but never offer us a ride, not even on the coldest of days.

"Don't walk too close to da road," Momma would always say.

Mr. Paul drove us to the port in Richmond to catch the cruise liner that would take us to Europe.

"You've got another think coming if you think for one second, I'm going to allow this dear child to spend her nights away from me down with them," shouted Miss Emily Barker at the captain who was being insistent that I could not stay in the cabin with her. "Well, how much would it cost to change your mind?" she offered after making a spectacle of herself in front of all the passengers for more than an hour.

"There's no amount of money that will make me change my mind about that, Madame!" said the captain, insulted by her offer. *Who the hell does she think she is?* he thought.

"I know there must be something that we can do to resolve this unfortunate situation. Would it be okay if she stayed with me as my assistant?" she said, pouring on the sweetness.

"Well, if you pay the extra for having your servant on board, then I guess that would be okay."

"Thank you, kind sir." *Bastard!* she thought.

"This is Angel. Her momma died a few years back. She doesn't have anyone to care for her, so I'm taking her under my wing. It's the least that I can do. Her family has worked for my family for as long as I can remember," Miss Emily Barker instinctually replied whenever anyone gave us a curious look. It always seemed to work. Most of the passengers would nod in approval, pat me on the head, and actually thank Miss Emily Barker for her kindness.

"They wouldn't understand it if we told them the truth, Angel dear. So I think that it's okay to tell this one little white lie, just this time . . ."

Little white lie! She was telling people that my momma was dead. That was more than a little white lie! But I still smiled all the same, although I was beginning to dislike Miss Emily Barker.

It wasn't like I was the only Negro passenger aboard the cruise liner. There were several Negro families making the trip to Europe as well. But even they looked at me funny. They didn't stay in the Whites Only section. *What she doing with dat white woman?* they thought.

Our cabin on the huge cruise liner was beautiful. There were two bedrooms, a real bathroom with running water, a toilet and tub, and even a sitting room with furnishings just as nice as those in Miss Emily Barker's home. Our cabin was bigger than the entire house that Momma and I lived in. My first night in the cabin felt like heaven. I slept in a soft, goose-feathered bed with crisp white linens.

We had breakfast in the beautifully decorated dining room every morning. "See, I told you, honey. This is what our lives are going to be like forever," she'd say whenever she saw me smiling about some new experience.

"Thank you, Miss Emily. You are so nice to me . . ." I said before being abruptly interrupted by her barking at the young colored boy who served us.

"Hey boy, I thought I told you yesterday that I wanted fresh strawberries with our breakfast this morning!" Miss Emily Barker snapped, ignoring the appreciation that I'd begun to shower upon her only a second ago. The boy looked to be only a few years older than me and was visibly embarrassed by the blatant disrespect that Miss Emily Barker unleashed upon him. The dining room was full of guests. Miss Emily Barker had already made a stink the day before to force them to let me eat with her. The rest of the black passengers were taking their meals down below. Now, she was making things even worse. *Who is this uncultured person?* one of the ladies at the table next to us thought.

"Yes ma'am," the boy said politely, ensuring that he did not make eye contact with her.

"I want those strawberries, boy!" she barked. "Now!" she shouted, quieting the entire dining room enough to hear a pin drop. "Well, don't just stand there saying the same thing, boy. Go get the strawberries, now git!" she yelled, causing even more of the dining guests to look our way and the young boy to run out of the dining room.

"Yes, ma'am," he quietly said as he quickly disappeared into the kitchen, but not before giving me a quick glance . . . *No need for her to be so rude,* he thought.

Damn southerners, thought one of the women at another table not too far from ours.

"I don't know what this world is coming to. I sure do miss your momma taking care of me. I never had to worry about not getting what I wanted when she served me."

This was the beginning of a very long and embarrassing voyage with Miss Emily Barker. She seemed oblivious to how others perceived her, black and white alike. Nothing was ever good enough for her. She yelled and screamed at all the servants, presenting herself like an old Southern slave madam. I don't think she had any idea that this was 1953! It got so bad that I made any excuse I could think of so that I would not have to take my meals with her.

Momma always would say, "Money don't make folks no nicer. If anything, most of dem think it gives them the right to be nasty." She sure was right about Miss Emily Barker.

Nothing that came out of this woman's mouth was her true self. She'd say and do just about anything to get what she wanted. The only thing that she seemed to truly care about was being with my momma's husband, Ricky. She would sit in her room for hours writing him letters that were never sent. I would carefully sneak a look at her letters while she took her daily walks along the cruise liner deck.

My Darling Ricky,

I have waited a long time and endured much loneliness in the hopes that we could one day have a family and be together. I long to be in your arms again as we were when we first met in Germany. This time, I will nurse your heart and not your wounds as I did back then. Your love is all I need. You, Angel and I will have the perfect life here in Europe, away from the prejudices and injustices in the United States . . .

Love always, Em.

She planned to steal me and keep me forever. She was never going to let me see my momma again. I was not going to let that happen. I didn't know what to do, but I knew that she would not be allowed to get away with this.

Oh Momma, what have I done? Dear Lord, don't let my selfishness break my momma's heart. She loves me so much. I miss you so much, Momma! It feels like my heart's going to bleed out of my chest. Dear Lord, please forgive me and make a way to get me back to my momma. In Jesus' name, I prayed.

After what seemed like weeks on the open seas, we finally docked in Bremerhaven, Germany. It was more beautiful than I could ever have imagined. The harbor was filled with ships and cruise liners. Everything seemed perfectly orchestrated as people departed and arrived at the port. We were definitely in Miss Emily Barker's element. She seemed to speak German perfectly; easily transitioning from English to German as needed.

"How did you learn to speak German, Miss Emily?"

"Many years ago, as a high school graduation present, my daddy sent me and several of my closest friends on a European vacation for several months. I'd taken several languages while in school but I really became fluent as we traveled throughout Europe. My friends and I volunteered at the Army hospitals located along our travel routes, including Germany. That's where I met . . . oh never mind," she said abruptly, realizing she was talking too much.

"Young man! Please take our bags to the train shuttle!" she barked in German.

We took the long but scenic train ride from Bremerhaven to Frankfurt, Germany. I had never been on a train before and definitely had never seen anything as beautiful as Germany. The people were so nice. They seemed particularly nice to me, especially the small children on the train who had never seen a Negro child before.

We were sharing a railcar with a really nice German family. There were two girls, one about my age and one a little older, and their parents. Miss Emily Barker chatted with the couple off and on throughout the entire eight-hour ride. The girls and I couldn't talk to one another but we found ways to connect through lots of smiles and gestures. The younger girl seemed to be obsessed with my hair and my caramel-colored skin. After many hours of reluctance, she finally mustered up enough nerve to touch my bare arm. I'm not sure what she expected my skin to feel like but without me even having to read her thoughts, her expression indicated that she was pleasantly surprised. As she reached to touch my hair, her mother slapped her hand back.

"Nein, das ist nicht gut," her mother scolded, thinking it inappropriate for her to be so forward. While it really didn't bother me, I was touched by her mother's concern for me. Her consideration for my feelings was something I hadn't experienced when interacting with white people, not ever.

"Oh its okay, Angel don't mind, go ahead and touch her," Miss Emily Barker said, confirming her lack of understanding and consideration for anyone other than herself.

Who did Miss Emily Barker think I was? Something to be stared at, probed and prodded whenever anyone felt like it. This was the beginning of the end for me. I had to get away from this woman.

At the recommendation of the family who shared the railcar with us, we checked into a beautiful hotel in Frankfurt. This time, no one gave us any trouble about me staying there. In fact, no questions of any kind were asked about me traveling with Miss Emily Barker. The bellman stacked our luggage onto his shiny brass luggage rack and we entered the elevator just like everyone else. There were lots of people in the hotel, mostly white people but some Negroes as well. It was nice to be able to just blend in with everyone else. Never in my whole life had I felt this welcome, not anywhere. That is until Miss Emily Barker opened her mouth. "Is this the largest room you have? I specifically asked for a suite on one of the higher floors. I want to be able to see the city from my balcony," she screamed at the bellhop in German. German is a strong language. To me, everything sounds like an argument. But it sounded even more aggressive when Miss Emily Barker spoke it.

"No! This simply won't do!" she said. It seemed to me that she was really trying to impress me with her rude behavior. But I was not impressed. I was embarrassed by her. Like Aunt Adele would always say, "Some folks you can't take nowhere! They act a damn fool no matter where dey at . . . ."

Miss Emily Barker became so irate that we had to return to the lobby. We viewed several suites before she was satisfied. The one good thing that came out of the whole ordeal was the German family that we shared the railcar with were now down the hall from us. This allowed me to get away from Miss Emily Barker and play with the girls, Ingrid and Marta.

Once the girls had a chance to touch and feel my hair and skin, we three got along just fine. Their parents would allow me to visit with them while they were out sightseeing or shopping. This was a real treat for the girls because their parents kept such a close eye on them at all times. Ingrid said it had something to do with their older brother Hans who had died in the war. I could feel that there was heartache in the family even before she told me of her brother's death. Both Ingrid and Marta wore small lockets around their necks containing their brother Hans' photo. They would kiss the locket several times a day as I visited with them.

We'd sit out on the balcony for hours just staring at the beautiful scenery with the church steeple in the distance. Little Marta was never far from her sister's side. I could feel how much they loved each other. It reminded me of Charlie.

"Angel, do you know why the soldiers were here during the war?" Miss Emily Barker asked me as we had our dinner in the hotel suite. Once again, she had made a scene in the hotel dining room, resulting in the concierge insisting that we take our meals in our suite.

"Yes, we learned about it in school and I've been reading about it. Hitler was a bad man," I said.

"Yes, and he had a lot of people killed. Even the Klaus's older son because he would not become a German soldier. They even threatened to take Marta and Ingrid away when they were little more than babies. People can be so cruel."

What was she talking about? She was as mean and rude as they come! Did she really not see this in herself?

As I lay in bed that night, I thought about Hans, Ingrid and Marta, and fell asleep through my tears. Charlie and I never had a chance to be brother and sister in this world; I lost him before we could.

Yes, to lose a loved one is a sad thing. But you and I will always be connected, thought Charlie as he stared into my eyes at my bedside. Charlie was now no more than a figure with piercing eyes. *Don't be afraid, Angel. I just want you to know that you're not alone. Hold on a little while longer. You'll be with Momma again. Please tell Ingrid and Marta that Hans says, hello lil Lebkuchen. That's his pet name for them.*

I closed my eyes for only a second, took a deep breath and he was gone . . .

"Oh Charlie, don't go! Please stay here with me. I haven't seen you in such a long time. I feel so alone . . ." I cried out through my tears.

It was a day just like any other day. I woke up to Miss Emily Barker laughing, almost giggling. "I am so glad that you found us. I thought I was going to have to stay here forever. What took you so long, my love?"

Who was she talking to?

"Oh, Ricky, oh Ricky, yes my love," she cried in ecstasy. "Yes my love," she cooed in unison with the sound of his grunts.

Well, there was no need to guess who had finally found us or what they were doing. With all pretenses gone, there was no need to hide their desire for one another, not even for my sake I guess. Disgusted by it all, I decided to just start breakfast without her. What a welcome treat this would be.

"Good morning, Angel, look who has just arrived!" said Miss Emily Barker, as she and my momma's husband Ricky joined me for lunch after being in bed for hours.

"Good morning," was all I could muster.

"Hi Miss Angel. How are you?" said my momma's husband Ricky.

"He has come a long way to visit with us," Miss Emily Barker said, grabbing his thigh right in front of me.

Visit! Who's she kidding? I thought.

"Em, this ain't no child no more. No need to start down this road lying to her. Miss Angel, your momma and I didn't get along as well as I hoped. She didn't much like the fact that I knew Em before her and she kicked me out of the house. So, here I am," said Ricky, offering me the lie that was obviously orchestrated by Miss Emily Barker. *Dis child ain't never gonna believe this shit!* he thought.

"I'm sorry to hear that. How is my momma?" was all I could muster once again.

"She fine."

"This is such a special day! Ricky is here and I have something for you as well, dear. I received a telegram yesterday from your momma! She wants you to know that she loves you and plans to join us real soon, dear," lied Miss Emily Barker as she waved the envelope in front of me then quickly placed it in her robe pocket just as I reached for it.

"Angel dear, Ricky and I are going to spend a little time together. Do you think you could spend the day with Ingrid and Marta?" Miss Emily Barker asked before I could respond to her lie about my momma.

"Yes ma'am." *Anything to get away from you two devils*, I thought.

I missed my momma so much. I missed her beautiful smile. Just thinking of the joy in her face whenever she told me that she loved me, now made my heart ache. Miss Emily Barker had stolen that smile and that love from me. I was a stupid girl, thinking so little of the love that my mother showered on me, taking for granted what she gave to me so freely. How stupid I was to think that such a love could be replaced with pretty dresses and a trip around the world.

Oh Momma! I know how much you wanted to have a family. Miss Emily Barker has stolen everything from you. Please Momma, please hold on. I'm coming. I won't let her take everything from you. I just won't. I love you, Momma. I miss you so much, Momma. Dear Lord, I have been stupid. Please Lord, take pity on me and help me find my way back to Momma, I prayed as I made my way down the hall. *All I want is to be in my momma's arms once again.*

Just as I was about to knock at the door, Ingrid and Marta opened the door to their suite. "Morgen," Ingrid said softly. "Today not good day," she added with tears in her eyes. Es ist Hans' birthday. Mother and Father are at cemetery. Not let Marta and I go," she cried, falling into my arms.

"I'm so sorry, Ingrid," I said as I followed her out to the balcony to join Marta. They stood at the railed edge looking out at the same scenery that we'd shared for months now. I sat in a small chair closer to the door crying. My tears were for Momma as much as they were for Ingrid and Marta. *Thank you Lord for this day. Allowing me to have this moment. Your ways are not my ways but they are always perfect.* We silently spent the rest of the day in each other's company.

The next morning, I was awakened to more noise. At first, I thought it was my momma's husband Ricky and Miss Emily Barker doing what they had been doing ever since the day he arrived, but not this time. It was the busy noise of bags being packed.

"Time to go," said Miss Emily Barker as she entered my bedroom without knocking.

"Where, ma'am?"

"Italy! We've decided to go to Italy!" she gleefully announced.

What? I can't go to Italy! Ingrid and Marta need me! I thought. "Can I say goodbye to my friends before we leave?" I calmly asked.

"Yes, but you'll have to hurry! We leave in two hours, you haven't had your breakfast and you aren't dressed yet."

"Yes, ma'am," I said, popping out of bed as fast as I could. Momma had always made me put my clothes out the night before. "Ya never knew know when you might need to git dressed in a hurry," she'd always say. *Thank you, Momma.* I was dressed and down the hall in five minutes.

"I'm so sorry. We're leaving today."

"Not ever see you again," the girls cried as we clung to one another.

"Please don't cry. We've had fun together haven't we? And I will never forget you. We can write each other. Please give me your address. I have something to tell you and you can't be scared," I struggled to say through the steady thumping of my heart.

"I not understand," said Ingrid as Marta ran to her bedroom crying uncontrollably.

"I have a message from Hans that came to me last night, in a dream . . ." To tell her any more than that would have been too much.

"He said to tell his two Lebkuchen hello."

"He always called us that. His little cookies – Lebkuchens," Ingrid said calmly. Thank you. I am glad to know that he is okay now. He died saving us. German soldiers shot him as he hid us under the gazebo in our garden. He gave his life for us. Mother and Father keep us close since then. You are the only one they trust. We will miss you. Hans was always smart. If he comes to you, means you good person. Danke for being our friend. We are friends for life." We hugged once more with the sounds of Marta crying her eyes out in the background.

"Auf Wiedersehen, Ingrid!" I said; my best attempt to speak German. "Auf Wiedersehen, Marta," I called out as I closed the door and ran back down the hall, knowing that I would never see them again.

Now I had to accept the fact that I had selfishly made a decision that would hurt my momma to her very core. She had dedicated her entire life to me and I had taken it for granted. At times, I was even embarrassed of her; preferring Miss Emily Barker's company over hers! Momma was a simple woman with simple desires and dreams and I wanted a more refined life. The life that Miss Emily Barker kept saying she could give me. She promised me that a better one was possible, even for a young Negro girl such as myself. She never really came right out and said it, although she implied a thousand times that Momma would never be able to teach me what I needed to really make it in this rapidly changing world where colored people were beginning to stand up for themselves and demand their civil rights. Some of us passively lived as we always had, while others were being spat on, beaten and hung up in trees as we continued to silently fight, following the teaching of Reverend Dr. Martin Luther King.

Everything was changing now. And not just because I was seeing more of the world. Colored folks were changing. We were getting bold. No matter what white folks did to us. We still kept pressing forward, no matter how scared we were. It was a strange time. I wasn't sure what we were calling ourselves from one month to the next.

"It don't make no difference what dey call us. Dey still treating us like slaves," Momma would say after a hard day of being at Miss Emily Barker's beck and call. "First we were called niggers, then Negroes and now colored." I decided that it didn't make a bit of difference what we were called. I just wanted to be able to live a life free to have my dreams come true.

It's sad to say, but to me, it felt like many of the colored people, especially the women, were following him not only for his teaching but also for his looks. Folks say he made no apologies about the fact that he was good looking. You only had to see him in the newspapers even while he was locked up in jail to understand why.

"That's one fine-ass Alabama preacher!" Aunt Adele would shout whenever anyone mentioned his name. I could always count on Aunt Adele to say exactly what other people were thinking but didn't have the nerve to say. I would give anything to be in my momma's little kitchen right now, eating Sunday dinner with the two of them, laughing so hard at the stories they told. Sometimes, we'd spend the whole afternoon sitting in our little kitchen.

Momma was grateful for everything that Aunt Adele had done to help us over the years but she never forgave her for treating Aunt Sissy so badly. That was the one thing that really kept Momma from truly forgiving her and loving Aunt Adele the way she so desperately needed. It wasn't Aunt Adele's fault that Granddaddy had tricked them both. He had both my momma's momma and Aunt Adele having babies for him at the same time. Funny how things can happen early in a person's life and they never get past it. It was as if they were in limbo, stuck in the same scene, replaying the same lines over and over again.

I never thought I'd ever say it, but I missed my life in Virginia. I even missed being in school, minus the mean kids of course. I missed my momma and Aunt Adele so much. Yes, I even missed Aunt Adele. I'd heard all the awful stories about her for most of my life. The stories that women and men alike talked about out loud and the ones they whispered when they thought no one could hear.

And now I found myself lost and totally dependent upon Miss Emily Barker. Just the way she wanted it. Once again, we were on the train. This time, it was my momma's husband Ricky, Miss Emily Barker and me traveling together impersonating a family.

We departed the train in a little town called Vicenza about an hour from Venice, Italy. Ricky had been taken to the hospital there when he was wounded during the war. It was a quaint little town, with cobblestone streets lined with small shops. Just like Germany, the people were really nice and no one seemed a bit bothered by the fact that we were colored.

We rented an apartment in town that provided breathtaking views of the town square. The Army base was only a few miles away. The apartment had more bedrooms than we could possibly use. Miss Emily insisted that she needed her space, just in case we had guests. She hired a nanny to care for me and act as my teacher.

Gretchen was German and had moved to Italy during the war to be with her husband, an American soldier. She spoke three languages, German—her native language—Italian and English. She was teaching German and Italian to the newly arrived soldiers and their families when Miss Emily Barker discovered her. Ricky thought she was perfect for me. The deal was sealed when Gretchen mentioned that her husband, a Negro soldier, had been killed in action. She had no children and neither her side nor her husband's side of the family had approved of their marriage.

Gretchen received Army survivor's benefits but it wasn't enough to cover all of her living expenses. Hence, becoming a nanny, teacher and surrogate mother to me seemed the right thing to do. We got along right away. Plus we instantly had one thing in common: Neither one of us liked Miss Emily Barker.

"I expect you to spend all of your time with our Angel. My husband and I will be attending lots of social events and we need to be able to depend on you to keep our Angel safe," Miss Emily Barker said, continuing the lie that she'd become so accustomed to telling.

"Of course," said Gretchen as she stretched out her arms to greet me for the first time. Gretchen was a huge woman, tall and big.

When she hugged me, it felt as if I disappeared in her arms. Her hugs reminded me of my momma. I could feel her heartbeat, and there was comfort in that.

"Glad to see you two bonding so well. Ricky and I will be going out tonight. Gretchen, consider tonight to be your probationary period," said Miss Emily Barker on the very first night Gretchen arrived.

"Of course," repeated Gretchen. *I really don't like this bitch and who does she think she's fooling? No ring on either one of their fingers. This child no look like either one of them.*

"Angel, you know that we can't tell Gretchen the truth about our family," said Miss Emily Barker the next morning.

"Yes ma'am." *Family!*

"If you do, they will come and take you away."

Well, I don't want to be here anyway!

"They'll find out that your momma was supposed to join us and never came. They will put your momma away too." *Because that's what I'll tell them*, she thought.

"Yes ma'am."

"I'm sorry to say this, dear. I don't want to hurt you, my dear. But you have to understand what will happen," she said slyly as she repositioned my braids, placing them over my shoulder with a disgusted look on her face as if she was picking up lint from the floor. *We have to do something about this nappy hair*, she thought.

"Yes, Miss Emily, I understand. I won't say anything . . ."

"Okay then, it's settled. I'll let Gretchen know that her employment with us officially starts tomorrow. We can put her in the room down the hall, closest to your room."

Now that Gretchen was with us, I saw very little of my momma's husband Ricky or Miss Emily Barker. Usually, they were already out of the house before Gretchen and I had our breakfast. Sometimes, they would be away for several days, sightseeing in the nearby towns. Each day would start the same when they were home.

"Yes. Yes. Yes, my love. Don't stop. Yes. Yes, almost, baby. Yes. Yes, Oh Yes!" Miss Emily Barker not so silently whispered until it was over.

"Promise me that you'll never leave me," she'd plead afterwards.

"I'm not going anywhere," Ricky would lie. *This bitch is crazy. She really think I'ma let her keep me like this. Her sex boy!*

"Ricky, my love. What's wrong?" she instinctually responded.

"Nothing, love," he said quietly.

'What? Tell me, love," she begged as she ran her fingers through the thick rug of hair on his chest.

"Why do you always say that?"

"Say what?"

"Ask me not to leave you?"

"Because, in the past, everyone has left me, my love. Daddy made sure of that. He gave me all this money and then made it so that I could never share it with anyone."

"Why would he do that?"

"Because he hated Mommy."

"Why did he hate his wife and the mother of his child?"

"Their marriage was arranged. Mommy was beautiful but Daddy said that she was spoiled and unloving. Mommy's parents were very religious. She'd been raised to believe that loving someone should only occur when you want to make a baby. She almost died trying to have me. She didn't want any more children after me. 'Some men's nature is way too high. A proper, God-fearing woman does not partake in the things that my husband wants me to do' I'd hear her confide in the ladies as they had their tea. That's why he'd leave us and go to Baltimore for extended periods of time to work with the Andersons. Lord only knows what else he was doing while he was there!"

"Who are the Andersons?"

"My daddy's best friend from childhood and his wife. Folks say Daddy was supposed to marry her but her family made her marry Mr. Anderson instead. The Anderson family was from old money, so Daddy never stood a chance."

"Is it really always about money?" Ricky spurted out without thinking.

"Money makes the world go round. At least that's what my Daddy would always say."

20

"Well, I don't have two nickels to rub together, so . . ."

"This is different, my love," she quickly interrupted him.

"How?"

"We belong to one another," she said, taking his manhood into her mouth as she always did when they had this discussion. Maybe this might have worked in the past, but the newness of these sexual experiences was quickly wearing off to the point that it was now becoming offensive to Ricky. *Am I so gullible that she thinks that I can be controlled by this? What the hell is she talking about?* Ricky thought as he lay back until she stopped.

"There you go, my love," Miss Emily Barker would say, feeling accomplished at her ability to please him.

I didn't really understand much of what any of this meant. But still, I could hear my momma's husband Ricky's thoughts. Thoughts that I wished I weren't able to hear. Thoughts that I was sure were for grown folks' ears only.

It was a day just like another day. Miss Emily Barker and my momma's husband Ricky were at it again, louder than ever before. I couldn't help but hear them through the sounds of the bed creaking as they moved in unison, causing me to feel something deep inside of myself. As the sounds got louder and faster, I felt my body reacting to it. I instinctually placed my hands on my private parts and discovered a dampness as if I'd just taken a bath.

The sounds they made lingered in my head, excited me, and caused my legs to tremble, my breathing to deepen, and placed me mentally at a place not far from their passion. I tried not to listen, not to allow my body to come alive, disgusted at myself for allowing it to happen. They were close to finishing now; I could tell by the speed by which the bed moved and the escalation of their moans. There in my bed, I silently and secretly joined in on their lustful, filthy acts; feeling alive but lonely; disgusted but renewed by this newfound physical release.

"Angel, you look different," Gretchen said after many nights of privately including myself in the escapades of Miss Emily Barker and my momma's husband Ricky.

"You're starting to look like a woman now. Time to buy you some proper undergarments, ja?" Gretchen said in her thick German accent.

It was true, in just a few short months, my breasts had progressed from being little, embarrassing pointed things under my blouse into two large breasts with nipples the size of quarters. Miss Emily Barker hadn't noticed and I wasn't about to ask her for anything more than was absolutely necessary.

I truly appreciated Gretchen's attention, although I knew that becoming a woman and learning how to take care of myself was something that my momma should be teaching me. Just the thought of all the experiences that Momma and I were missing caused me to miss her even more.

I had spent two birthdays away from Momma now. I knew that she didn't have the money to come get me. I wasn't even sure if she knew where I was. Someday, I was going to have to do it on my own. I'd just leave. The longer that I was away from Momma, the cloudier my thoughts became. The spirits were no longer visiting me at night and somehow I was sure that was not a good thing. I was alone now. Alone, without even the scary eyed souls to guide me.

Just Ain't Right

"That child ain't never gonna be happy without her momma," Ricky said to Miss Emily Barker after she completed the sexual acts that she always used to get her way.

"What can her momma give her that we can't, my love?"

You have a lot to learn about matters of the heart. You don't have a clue! Ricky thought. "And what do you think that her momma gonna do? She ain't gonna just let you take the one thing that she has without even putting up a fight," Ricky said.

"It's not fair that she should have a beautiful, smart, sweet child like Angel and I have nothing."

"But you have me, my love," Ricky said, thinking it might soften her up.

"But I want a family! I want us to be a family!" she screamed like the small, spoiled child that she was.

"We don't need a child to be a family. Plus we could both end up in jail if we don't figure something out and soon."

"You act as if I stole the child. Angel came with me on her own accord."

"Now, you know that she ain't old enough to make those kinda decisions for herself."

"Oh, you don't know my Angel then!"

"Well, the law say different." *And I ain't going to jail for your crazy ass. You'll smile and they gonna pat you on the back. Maybe give you fine. But me, my black ass they gonna throw in the jail or worse as soon as they find out we sleeping together*, Ricky thought.

"Don't you want us to be a family?"

"Of course I do!" Ricky lied. *Oh shit! Here we go.*

"I've done all of this for you, my love," Miss Emily Barker cried, repeating the same old lines that she would always say whenever Ricky backed her in a corner. "What do you want me to do?"

"For starters, my love, we need to figure out a way to stop Georgie from sending the police to fetch her daughter!"

"Don't you ever speak her name in our bed!" screamed Miss Emily Barker. "Sometimes it seems that you care for her more than me. Why are you so concerned about what that country, uncultured, nigg . . ." She stopped just before finishing.

Woo now, you done gone too far! My momma always would say, eventually they gone call you a nigger. This was not the beautiful, young, compassionate young girl with the crystal blue eyes that he'd met so many years ago. The girl who gladly accepted the ridicule and stares that she received daily with each visit that she made to the Army hospital. The girl who delayed traveling throughout Europe with her friends to care for him.

Miss Emily Barker, Em as Ricky called her, would visit him every day, just to hold his hand. Her deep blue eyes and smiles guided him through the pain that was the result of the multiple bullets that ravaged his body when his platoon was ambushed. The doctors were able to remove some of the bullets, but not all of them. One bullet was so close to his heart, they were afraid to even try to remove it. But Em's care and her love acted like a shield around his heart, protecting him from harm.

Eventually, the handholding turned into kisses on his forehead, his eyes and then lingering on his lips. She swore that if Ricky kept fighting, she would never leave his side. Em could never possess the evil that was spewing out of the woman he saw before him today.

"I never could stand her. No matter what came her way, she was always smiling and praying and hoping. Well, how's that working for you now, Georgie?" she said, full of spite.

All this time, I thought that she wanted a family but underneath it all was the fact that Em was just plain jealous of a woman who had damn near nothing, but everything as far as Em was concerned. Damn shame what pure jealously and hatred can do to a person,

Ricky thought as he pretended to console her by stroking her hair as she cried in his arms.

"Hey, maybe we can send her some money," she said as she quickly recovered from her crying spell. "Daddy always said money could cure almost anything. I'll call my lawyers in Baltimore later today," she announced.

Ricky didn't say a word as he lay there disgusted and ashamed of himself for being a part of Miss Emily Barker's plot.

I'm so sorry, my sweet Georgie. You really don't deserve any of this. I'm so sorry to have had any part in this. Please forgive me. I gotta let you know that I'm sorry. I don't give a damn what Em think. I'ma find a way to write you and tell you how sorry I really am. Lord, please forgive me, Ricky prayed as he drifted off to sleep.

Not This Time!

I can feel Ricky slipping away from me like so many others before him. Daddy would always say that no real man would be able to stay with me unless he had money of his own. To drive that point home, Daddy arranged for my dowry to arrive like clockwork each month as long as I was married to someone who had as much money as he had left me or remained unmarried and childless.

Well, you're not going to win, Daddy! You made Mommy's life a living hell. You slept with other women right in the bedroom next to the one you shared with her. There's no way that I'm going to let control my life from your grave! The first time you caught me kissing a boy under the big tree in our front yard, you had me strung up behind the smokehouse and whipped me until my clothes fell off. I was only fourteen. You wanted to hurt Mommy, humiliate me, and scare away any decent boy. Oh! You were a master at controlling everything and everyone around you.

Mommy was too weak to stop you and you would just buy off anyone else who tried. I thought I was rid of you when your brand new shiny car, the first in the county, got swept away in the flood, with you and Mommy in it.

Well, I'm not going to let you take Ricky and Angel away from me. I'm going to fight you, Daddy, Miss Emily Barker thought as she slipped out of the bed that she shared with Ricky and quickly got dressed.

That beating Daddy gave me would have probably been even worse if he'd known that I was with child. The father was one of our Negro workers. Something about his dark skin had always attracted me. The thought that Daddy would have a heart attack if he ever caught me with my legs wrapped around one of his Negro workers only added to the excitement of laying with a Negro man.

I didn't even really like ole Edward. He was nothing special. Dumb as a doornail! He was scared to death the first time I seduced him.

Daddy beat me so bad that I lost the baby and the complications from it made it so that I could never have another child. Daddy would have loved it if he could have thrown that in my face. But Mommy took our secret to her grave. She wasn't as soft as she pretended to be when Daddy was around. She gave me something to drink made from pine tree bark that had me throwing up for days. Then Mommy took me to see the doctor while Daddy was on one of his whoring trips to Baltimore. That's what Mommy called his trips when she had high tea with her lady friends.

Doctor said all the trauma was too much and that I'd never be able to conceive again. The hatred I felt for my daddy was so strong that I dreamed of killing him in his sleep. I knew Mommy wouldn't survive it. So I would pretend he didn't exist. I've been fighting his hold on my life for what seems like forever.

It didn't take Miss Emily Barker very long to make all the arrangements required to send Momma a $100 check each month. Again she lied to her benefactors to schedule the monthly check.

"That is a lot of money, Miss Emily. May I ask why you are sending this Negro woman so much money?"

"No, you may not. This is my money and I'll do with it as I please. You have made it clear what the stipulations of my dowry are and this request is not in conflict with it, so do it!" she yelled at him through the phone. $100 was peanuts as far as she was concerned.

That should keep that stupid bitch quiet, she thought as she returned to the hotel suite, happy to be in control once again.

Venezia

I would spend another birthday away from my momma. Seeing the world did not lessen the heartache of being without her. So much had happened. I wondered if Momma would be able to endure my absence. Miss Emily Barker kept up the lie that my momma was coming to join us by pretending to receive letters from Momma:

"Look what I have for you, Angel dear," said Miss Emily Barker as she pretended to read a letter while we caught the ferry over to Venice for the weekend. "Your momma still loves you so very much and cannot wait to join us. She needs to save a little more money. I've offered to pay her expenses but you know that she won't hear of it. Seems silly to me. If it were me, I would swallow my pride to be with you, Angel dear," said Miss Emily Barker, stabbing her lie into my heart in an attempt to discredit my momma.

"Yes ma'am," was all that I could manage to say once again. I was so tempted to ask to read the letter and end this lie once and for all. But what good would that do? I'd seen how vindictive and downright mean Miss Emily Barker could be. I had to be smart in making my escape.

Venice was beautiful. I was grateful to be able to see it with Gretchen, away from my momma's husband Ricky and Miss Emily Barker. Our apartment was only a few hours away, but Miss Emily Barker had to do everything on a grand scale, so we reserved a double deluxe suite in one of the most famous and luxurious hotels in Venice, only a few steps away from St. Mark's Square. From our suite, we could see a sea of gondolas waiting to shuttle us anywhere we wanted to go along the infamous canals that formed a maze in the city.

As soon as we were checked into the hotel, the two of them were off doing God knew what. Miss Emily Barker arranged a line of credit accessible to Gretchen through the front desk and we were left alone to do whatever we wanted.

Gretchen would always make me complete my studies before our outings. "A woman needs to be able to take care of herself in this world and nothing opens doors like a good education," she'd say, sounding just like my momma. We were just about to leave for our evening walk when the telephone rang.

"Gretchen, Ricky and I are in the hotel dining room. We want to celebrate Angel's birthday. Could you make sure that she's dressed appropriately? I want the two of you to meet us downstairs as soon as possible," she ordered, hanging up the telephone before Gretchen could respond. This was the first mention of my birthday made by Miss Emily Barker. As usual, she and my momma's husband Ricky had left before I awakened.

"Well, birthday girl, it looks like you're going to get your chance to dress up," Gretchen said sarcastically. "We will dine downstairs tonight," she announced with a tad too much enthusiasm to sound sincere.

"Birthday girl! Nope! I'm a woman now," I proudly announced.

"No, you're not. Not yet!" Gretchen said sternly as she placed the garment bag on my bed containing my new outfit that we'd fought so fiercely about purchasing. Lately, I didn't know what was going on with me. Even Gretchen and I weren't getting along. I wanted to look like Dorothy Dandridge with her hourglass figure. I thought she was the most beautiful colored woman that I had ever seen. The Europeans loved her and she was doing very well in the movies. Dorothy Dandridge was the first Negro woman to be nominated for an Academy Award and I wanted to look just like her. So, when I saw the dress in the shop window with a sign that read, *Like the dress worn by Dorothy Dandridge in the movie Carmen Jones*, I just had to have it.

I wanted to wear the latest fashions. I had inherited the best parts of both my momma and the man that they said was my daddy, although he had never spoken a single word to me. Momma's chest and his height and his straight, bright white teeth. My teeth had gotten me out of a lot of arguments with Gretchen. Whenever it seemed that she would not budge, I'd give her a big smile and she'd melt like butter. But not this time.

"Miss Emily will fire me for sure if I allow you to buy this." Gretchen said, holding the dress away from her like a smelly dish rag.

But I was sold on the dress from the moment I tried it on. There is just something about a well-made garment. You can just tell right away when it fits well. I proudly walked out of the dressing area and stood in front of the three-sided floor length mirror for Gretchen and all the other ladies in the store to see. Everyone in the store turned in my direction, confirming that I had made the right choice. Gretchen still thought that the dress was too much for a girl my age but she gave into my pleading and the compliments made by everyone in the store.

"All the girls are wearing this, plus I'm sixteen and a woman now. You are so old fashioned," I snapped.

"Not yet you're not. Just because you can wear the dress, doesn't mean you should. Plus. I don't think I like your tone!" she said, ensuring that I knew that she wasn't happy with my choice.

"I'm sorry," I said with the biggest smile I could muster.

"I will allow it this time only because it's your birthday. But if Miss Emily says that you have to return it, then that's what we'll do. No argument, ja?"

"Yes, Frau Gretchen, thank you." *Yes Momma*, I thought.

So when Miss Emily Barker requested our presence for dinner, I was more than ready to comply with her demand. For once, I was even excited to have dinner with them, looking like the woman that I so wanted to be.

Making Me Nervous

We received similar stares as we entered the dining room to meet Miss Emily and Ricky. All eyes seemed transfixed on us. Well, on me actually. It was the first time that I felt admired by so many people. Everyone in the dining room seemed to pause for a moment as Gretchen and I made our way to the table.

My outfit was perfect. The pale blue dress was ideal for my caramel complexion. My tiny waist and fully developed figure allowed me to give Ms. Dorothy Dandridge a run for her money.

As we looked around the dining room for Miss Emily Barker and my momma's husband Ricky, several couples at nearby tables nodded their approval. If only I could hear their thoughts, but my gift was fading more and more each day.

As we drew near the table located toward the back of the dining room, I could see that Miss Emily and my momma's husband Ricky were not alone. There was another couple with them. A handsome man with a Dick-Tracy-like chin, olive-colored skin, and perfectly placed hair that was graying around the temples was sitting there with one of the most beautiful women that I think I have ever seen. Her features were striking. Light brown eyes, thin nose, and lips so small that they looked like the lips on one of my baby dolls. Both Ricky and the man stood as we neared the table. The tall man seemed to stumble a bit as he stood. The beautiful lady seemed immediately annoyed.

"My, my, my! Who is this lovely young lady?" the distinguished man said before being properly introduced.

"Angel dear, you look lovely. Happy birthday, my dear," Miss

Emily Barker said as she kissed me on both cheeks, European-style. "Let me introduce to you my long-time dear friend of the family, Mr. John Anderson and his friend Regina. This is our adopted daughter."

"Hello! Well, she sure is a pretty lil thang!" Mr. Anderson immediately said, holding my chair out for me as he melted my clothes off with his eyes.

"Hello everyone," I said as Gretchen pulled out the chair beside me, although she was never introduced.

"How lovely you are! Isn't she, Regina? She reminds me of you when you were her age," said Mr. Anderson. This was the start of a dinner filled with compliments, stares and moments of uncomfortable silence brought on by the overly attentive Mr. Anderson. The more attention Mr. Anderson showered on me, the more irritated Miss Regina became.

"Well . . . you have done a fine job with this one. She is going to make some young man extremely happy." He beamed as Ricky stared him down. "We must celebrate. Waiter! Give this little lady anything that her heart desires!" he said with so much emphasis on the word desire that Regina excused herself.

"Excuse me, while I find the ladies room," Regina said.

"Don't bother, Regina," snapped Mr. Anderson as he stumbled to his feet to assist her with her chair, resulting in yet another moment of uncomfortable silence. She may not have been able to read his mind but she made it known that she recognized she was suddenly not the center of attention.

As soon as Regina was far enough away not to hear and unmoved by her irritation, Mr. Anderson took full advantage of the opportunity to inquire more about me. I didn't think Regina had quite made it to the ladies room before Mr. Anderson boldly made his interest in me known to everyone still at the table.

"You are going to make one fine woman. So, how old are you, dear?" Mr. Anderson asked.

"I told you, silly. Today is my lil Angel's sixteenth birthday," teased Miss Emily Barker.

"John, I see that you haven't changed a bit!" said Miss Emily Barker. "You are just as smooth as ever. My daddy never really got over you stealing your late wife from him, God rest her soul." This was followed by another moment of uncomfortable silence.

"Well, Regina wasn't much older than your lil Angel when . . ." John hesitated to finish a statement that was way too inappropriate in my presence.

What the hell did he just say? my momma's husband Ricky thought. *Sick bastard!* This was the first time in months that I could hear anyone's thoughts.

There's something about you, dear, that feels so familiar," he continued as Regina approached the table.

"Thank you," said Regina as my momma's husband Ricky quickly stood up to hold her chair out for her. He too was finding it impossible not to be intoxicated by her French perfume and her freshly washed hair that smelled like jasmine.

"You're welcome, Miss Regina." *Woo Wee!*

"That's my Ricky," Miss Emily Barker said with as much sarcasm as she could muster. "Always so polite!"

"Ma'am, Angel has much schoolwork tomorrow. Think we should leave now," Gretchen said, breaking the silence.

"Oh no! Can't we stay just a little longer?" I pleaded, enjoying being the center of attention even if it was coming from a man old enough to be my daddy. It's my birthday and I'm sixteen now, almost a woman!"

"Yes," said Mr. Anderson, quickly concurring.

"You got some mo years ahead a you before you be a woman," Ricky said, breaking his silence for the evening.

"They're bringing the cake out now. You two can leave afterwards," said Miss Emily Barker, ignoring Ricky's disapproval of Mr. Anderson's behavior.

The cake was beautiful. Everyone in the restaurant sang *Happy Birthday* to me. Mr. Anderson and Miss Regina congratulated me by giving me a hug; with Mr. Anderson's hug being inappropriately too long, and Gretchen and I left very shortly afterwards.

"So where are you two staying?" asked Miss Emily Barker, once the goodbyes had been said to Angel and Gretchen.

"We arrived only yesterday. We're at the Omni just down the road," said Mr. Anderson.

"So are we! And we've got plenty of room. Oh, you just have to come stay with us. Right Ricky, dear? It would be so nice to be able to converse with Americans for a while," she continued without giving Ricky a chance to respond. "Plus Daddy, God rest his soul, would be quite upset if you and your lovely companion declined my invitation," said Miss Emily Barker.

"Companion!" Regina repeated, displaying her disdain for the insult.

"Oh, I'm sorry, dear. I know that we're all grown here. I just didn't want to offend you and I guess I failed in my attempt. I'm so sorry. Please forgive me," Miss Emily Barker said with an extra dose of insincerity.

"Um hum," said Regina as she rolled her eyes.

"Well, it's getting late. We should be heading home," interrupted Ricky.

"We'd love to stay with you all. It's no imposition." Mr. Anderson slyly smiled at the thought of seeing Angel once more.

"Great, then it's settled," said Miss Emily Barker as Ricky pulled her chair out for her.

The drive to the hotel was full of reminiscing between Miss Emily Barker and Mr. Anderson while Ricky and Regina pretended to be amused. Once again, Ricky was witnessing just how phony Miss Emily Barker truly was. Speaking so endearingly about her father. The same person whom she had only a few days earlier blamed for her mother-less, husband-less existence.

Angel had already retired by the time they arrived. Gretchen was quite surprised to see the four of them when she unlocked the top lock on the door to let them in. "Look who's going to be staying with us for a few days!" Miss Emily Barker announced. "Is the spare room at the end of the hall ready for guests?" she asked.

"Yes, ma'am," Gretchen replied, trying not to show her disapproval. She didn't like this Mr. Anderson character one bit.

"Great! Okay then. Goodnight you two," she said playfully, implying what she assumed would be going on in just a few minutes.

"I walk you to your room," said Gretchen as she led Mr. Anderson and Regina down the hall.

"What a beautiful suite," Regina said.

"Only the best for Miss Emily," Gretchen said just as they passed Angel's room. As usual, her door was slightly open. She was sprawled out among what seemed to be a thousand pillows of every shape and color. Her leg was hanging over the edge of the bed as if she could take off running at any time.

"If you should need anything, my room is last door further down the hall," Gretchen said as she quietly closed Angel's bedroom door. "Guten abend. Breakfast starts at 8 a.m. sharp."

"Thank you, dear," Mr. Anderson said as he placed his hand in the small of Regina's back, guiding her into their lavishly decorated room then closing the door behind them.

"Well, you sure did make an ass of yourself tonight!" Regina whispered as she removed Mr. Anderson's shoes, as she'd done for far too long.

"Regina, dear. What do you mean?"

"You know exactly what I mean. You were damn embarrassing. A man your age, drooling over that little girl."

"What girl?"

"Don't you what girl me! Don't forget who you talkin' to," Regina whispered. "I know your ass and all of your tricks!"

"Reginaaaa, please. I was only being nice."

"Oh, I know about you being nice. I remember you being nice to me like that when I was just about her age!"

"Please Regina. You know that you are and will always be the love of my life. Haven't I proved that to you time and time again? I would gladly give my life for you. Everything I have belongs to you. I thought I proved that when we sent my children to live with their grandparents, when I set up a line of credit so that you could have your own money, when I put Hazel in charge of the shop so that we could travel the world. I've done everything that you've asked. How could you think such a vile thing of me?"

"Um hum . . ." Regina softened. "Sometimes you just make me so mad, John. It's been a long day. We've been traveling for months. Maybe I'm just tired," Regina said, trying to defuse what was quickly turning into an argument. "I'm going to take a bath and just go to sleep."

But Regina couldn't sleep. Each time she tried to fall asleep, she had the sense that she was not alone. Mr. Anderson was snoring like a freight train but that wasn't the problem. She had learned to ignore him over the years they had been together.

Her thoughts were consumed by the gray figures that seemed to be popping in and out of her consciousness, making it impossible for her to drift off. They were unrecognizable spirits with voices that penetrated her thoughts without the use of sound, repeating the same thing over and over again as they stood at her bedside.

"Tell Georgie to hold on, this too shall pass."

What is this? Lord, please protect me, Regina prayed, until she finally fell asleep.

The following day started the same as it always did with Miss Emily Barker and my momma's husband going at it. I was determined that I would no longer join in on their filthy sexual sessions. Even if no one saw me, I knew it was wrong. It didn't matter one bit that I felt such a release and tingling afterward. This act was draining me of my second sight. I couldn't hear the thoughts of the people around me anymore. I needed my gift now more than ever. None of the people around me could be trusted, except for Gretchen of course.

"How well do you know this John Anderson?" Ricky asked Miss Emily Barker as they got ready for bed.

"I've known him since I was a child. Although it's been over twenty years since I saw him last," Miss Emily Barker said as she slipped back into her nightgown.

"I don't like him. I don't like how he looks at Angel," Ricky said and he felt his chest tighten as it filled with anger. Someone had to look out for this little girl cuz Em sure wasn't. Angel was just another pet. This fact was becoming more and more obvious to Ricky.

"Oh, Ricky! He's harmless. Plus Angel is just a child."

"She sixteen now and that never stopped men like him before! How long are they going to be staying with us? And why didn't you ask me before you invited them to stay? Or do you make all of the decisions round here?" *I'm really getting tired of you treating me like a child.*

"Of course not, dear! I just assumed that you would enjoy spending time with another couple like us."

"Like us! How are they like us? Oh, you think cuz she black and he white, dey like us! Is dat how you see us, me being you're traveling . . . Wait. What was the word you used? Oh yeah . . . companion. After all that we've been through, iz that what I am now, your traveling companion?" Ricky said as he attempted to catch his breath.

"Ricky! Of course not, dear. What's gotten into you?"

"You Em! You've gotten in to me! I don't like what I'm hearing."

"I'm sorry, my love. Look, it's been a long day. Let's just go to bed," she said, sliding her body against his as she pulled the covers up.

"No! What is wrong with you, Em?" Ricky said as he pushed her away from him and turned his back to her.

"I just want to love you, that's all," she said with blue eyes filled with tears.

"Let's just go to sleep," Ricky said as he tried to catch his breath and release the tightening in his chest.

"You okay, my love?"

"I'm fine."

"Time for breakfast," Gretchen said after knocking and then poking her head in my bedroom door. "Guten morgen, Mr. Anderson and Miss Regina," she said as they passed her in the hallway. "By the way, we have guests," she added to me.

"Morgen," said Mr. Anderson as he peeked his head into Angel's door. "Morning, Angel." He smiled, happy to have caught me wearing a short, thin cotton nightshirt that slightly showed off my thin body frame and huge perky breasts.

"Time for breakfast," Regina said as she almost pulled his arm out of its socket in her attempt to snap him out of his lustful, inappropriate thoughts.

"Hey!" exclaimed Mr. Anderson.

"Oh, I'm sorry, dear. I'm so hungry this morning," Regina lied as she smirked internally.

It was a day just like any other day. Everyone had finished eating breakfast. The itinerary was set for the day ahead. While Gretchen and I maintained our normal schedule of schoolwork, everyone else would be enjoying a day of shopping, sightseeing and dining. The only thing we had to look forward to was an afternoon walk in the park and I preferred to skip that.

After pleading with Gretchen for almost an hour, she allowed me to skip our regimen of visiting her friends along our walking route and return home for a nice quiet nap. With the house empty of guests, my thoughts were consumed with my desire for release and to satisfy my needs in private.

I was a young woman now with needs to be met. The thoughts that consumed me had nothing to do with the fact that I had been listening to Miss Emily Barker and my momma's husband Ricky going at it. This was my own passion. I was becoming a woman, not only physically but also mentally. I loved my momma but I would not live my life as she had, refusing to accept my sexuality, my desires, my longings. The year would be 1960 very soon. Times were changing and I was changing with them.

Just the thought of pleasuring myself hardened my nipples and caused my private parts to vibrate. I lay among the pillows and found my rhythm accompanied only by the thumping of my loose headboard that Gretchen had been promising to repair. The silence of the house and the solitude of my secret were such a treat. I felt my body easily reaching climax and knew that at any moment I would be there. My mind filled with dreams of the day when someone, anyone, would be pleasing me and there would be no need for this substitution for affection. How I prayed for the day when a man would make me feel like this. I could only imagine how much more satisfying that would be.

That's when I heard my bedroom door slowly open. "What a lovely young woman you are! How sad it is that you're alone and forced to pleasure yourself," he whispered, reading my thoughts. "Don't worry, I won't tell. I won't hurt you."

I could have screamed but what good would that have done? Plus I was almost there and so badly wanted to actually feel the touch of someone instead of secretly joining in with Miss Emily Barker and my momma's husband Ricky.

"I won't hurt you," he repeated. "I'm only here to help you, dear." There was that word, "dear" again. A sure indication of the lie he was trying fill my head with.

"May I?" he politely but seductively said as he reached for my breasts with the tips of his fingers. "Yes, this will be our little secret. I won't tell on you," he promised.

"Tell on me!" I may be only sixteen but I knew that he had it all wrong. This would be my secret to tell if I chose to. It would be him that would be in trouble, not me.

"Yes," he said as placed his warm tongue on my breast, causing me to quiver while guiding my hand in massaging my private parts.

"Don't worry, you'll be there in a moment, dear," he said as he knelt bedside my bed as if in prayer. He placed his tongue in my navel, causing an explosion inside of me so intense that all my previous pleasure sessions could not compare.

"May I?" he asked as he placed his tongue in the wetness I'd created, causing me to explode once again. This time, I was unable to contain my pleasure and screamed in delight.

"I won't tell," he said as he quietly exited my room, with only a slight thump made by his custom-made shoes as he recovered from being on his knees.

Is that what all the fuss was about? A few fleeting moments of pleasure. I had hoped that lovemaking would be so much more than this. In actuality, it was quite disappointing and I wondered why grown folk centered their whole life on it. This was nothing like the romantic scenes that I read about in the books that I secretly read whenever I had the chance. The one thing that seemed appealing was my ability to so easily excite this man. No, I wouldn't tell on him. In just the few moments that we shared, he confirmed that I possessed power. Power to control the feelings of another person, if only for a moment.

I sure hoped that there was more to lying with a man than what had occurred between me and Mr. Anderson. I wondered if Mr. Anderson's inability to cause sparks to fly was because he was so much older than me. Sure, it was my first time and it was more than I had been able to secretly do by myself, but still, I felt that something was missing.

I was beginning to understand what Aunt Adele would always say. "Ain't nothing an ole ass man can do for me but give me his money."

In The Minds of Men

Mr. Anderson returned to the bedroom that Emily had so graciously allowed him and Regina to share in total disgust with himself. He had allowed his pride and sexual desires to take control once again. There was no excuse for what he had allowed his passions to succumb to. He knew what would happen from the very first moment that he laid eyes on Angel. He just could not keep his eyes off her. There was something about this young black beauty that felt so familiar. He felt as if he had met her before although he knew that he had not.

Her skin was perfection. Her facial features striking. Brown eyes, so innocent to the world of experiences that she would someday have. Elongated nose with the cutest tip. Lips so full he found it difficult not to imagine what they would be like to kiss.

What the hell have I done? I'm lucky enough to have on my arm a woman that most men would die for. But in comparison to Angel, Regina seems average. What the hell? What's happening here? Never before have I thought of my lovely Regina in such a causal, unflattering way. Regina's taught me so much about the sensuality that consumes the essence of a colored women like no other woman in the universe.

Angel's just a child. To have such thoughts about her and to act upon them is just wrong. Reliving their brief encounter made his head spin. It was obvious that she knew very little and had been with no one else. The thought that he could be her first lover was all he could think of.

It is time for you to leave, the faceless figure beside the bed pierced into Mr. Anderson's thoughts. *It is time for you to leave,* it repeated into his semi-conscious state. He was somewhere between sleep and consciousness and unable to move.

"John!" Regina said, violently shaking him to awaken him. "I thought you said you'd meet me at the shop! I waited there for you for more than an hour! What is the matter with you?" she yelled.

"I'm so sorry, Regina. All of this traveling is wearing me down. I decided to catch a quick nap while you shopped. I guess I was more tired than I thought," he lied.

"Uh hum," she replied suspiciously. "Ricky and Em have invited us to dinner again tonight. You had better get dressed. I've laid your clothes out on the chair," she said as she disappeared into the bathroom.

"Thank you. You're so good to me," he replied through his guilt. One thing was for certain, it was time to leave. It's not every day a person experienced a haunting, and he was determined not to stay in that suite one more night.

"Regina and I would like to thank you for your hospitality," Mr. Anderson said as he looked down into his plate at dinner the following night. He did not make eye contact with Angel for the entire night. "We will be leaving for the US in the morning.

"Whaat? We were hoping that you two would stay for at least a few more days, weren't we, Ricky dear? It's been so nice having people in the house. Can't you stay a little longer?" Miss Emily Barker pleaded without allowing Ricky to speak.

"Da man know what's best," Ricky said through his coughing.

"But Ricky!"

"Em, stop!" Ricky said, louder than he ever spoke. In fact, it was loud enough to cause everyone at the table to become silent.

"Ricky!" Miss Emily Barker screamed as my momma's husband Ricky fell out of his chair and collapsed onto the floor. "Ricky! Gretchen call the doctor, something's wrong!" Gretchen was already dialing the phone.

"Hospital said that you should bring him to the emergency room immediately," Gretchen said as she helped a now silent Ricky back to his chair.

Something was definitely wrong and everyone at the table knew it. My momma's husband Ricky didn't look right. It looked as if the left side of his body had melted, starting with his almost closed eye, drooping lip, curled up arm and fingers, and his left foot turned inward.

Miss Emily Barker was hysterical. "Ricky, my dear Ricky. Please hold on," she said as the taxi driver helped place him in the car with her, Mr. Anderson and Regina climbing in the back seat.

"We'll call you from the hospital as soon as we can," Miss Emily Barker said to Gretchen through her tears. "Take care of my Angel," was all she said, never acknowledging me.

Later that night, Miss Emily Barker called from the hospital to tell us that Ricky had had a stroke brought on by the one bullet left near his heart. For the next few weeks, she spent every waking moment by his bedside just as she had done so many years ago.

After much pleading by Miss Emily Barker, Regina and Mr. Anderson agreed to stay with us for an additional week. Mr. Anderson kept his distance from me. After a few days, I began to think that maybe I had made up our encounter. That it really had not happened at all.

"May I come in?" he whispered as he knocked on my bedroom door, slightly opening it. "Gretchen and Emily are saying their goodbyes to Regina at the taxi. I want you to know that I am truly sorry for my behavior, Miss Angel." No one had ever called me that.

"I want you to know that I think very highly of you. You are a lovely young woman and I let my lustful desires get the best of me that beautiful night. I hope that you can find it in your heart to forgive me. Should ever you need anything, please do not hesitate to ask me," Mr. Anderson said as he handed me a small sealed envelope containing his address in Baltimore. "I hope that you will not be offended by the contents of this," he said. "I only want to take care of you in any way that you will allow me to." *I love you my sweet,* he thought, making my heart pound and the tips of my fingers tingle. No man had ever said, or should I say thought this about me before.

"Thank you," was all that I could say as he exited my bedroom, the house and my life.

*

Angel needed more than Gretchen was able to give her. The older she became, the more abrasive she was toward her. This girl needed to be with a family that would look out for her. Not just drag her around the world being cared for by only a nanny. Gretchen was beginning to feel that she had gotten in over her head. Helping her with her studies was one thing but to be her surrogate mother was not what she'd signed up for. Angel needed more care than Gretchen was able to give, and she wanted to return to Germany and try to reconcile with her own family.

Her late husband David was a good man but her family hated the fact that he'd taken Gretchen away from them. Before David came along, her family had never even met a Negro before. Their only exposure to Negroes was what they saw on the television. They were scared for their daughter. The world was changing but the violence between the races in America was something that they did not want her to be a part of. Their greatest fear was that Gretchen would follow her husband to America and be killed or worse.

Gretchen had dreamed of going to America her entire life. Her Uncle Hendrik would tell her brothers, sisters and Gretchen stories about the business trips he made to America before the war. Never in any of his stories was there mention of colored people.

When Gretchen met David at a dance on the Army post, she was sure that she'd met Sidney Poitier. He was tall, dark and handsome and Gretchen thought he was the most beautiful man that she'd ever seen. He had a certain shyness about him. David said that his momma had taught him to be respectful of women and treat them with dignity and respect.

The first time they kissed, she kissed him. To this day, she was sure they wouldn't have kissed if she hadn't. She saw David as a beautiful man and he saw her as a white girl that he wasn't allowed to look at, let alone touch. It didn't matter to him one bit that Gretchen was German. To him, she was a white woman. No different from the white women in America, off limits, "Unless ya wanna be hanging from a tree," he would say. David was from a little small town called Many, Louisiana. The town had a history of slavery.

When the first census was taken in 1850, the population consisted of 3,347 whites and 1,168 slaves. And old ways die hard.

Gretchen was only nineteen when they met. Her mother would always say that she was older than her years. Back then, people would say that she was pretty, with long blond wavy hair that reached her waist. She was tall but quite thin back then due to all the work she did on the farm. Her three sisters and four brothers spent most of their days helping Papa run the farm or getting their education through Mother who was a teacher before she married Papa. Gretchen never really had a problem with her weight until after David was killed. He was everything to her and when he died, she had no reason to care about her appearance. She missed his touch and the way he'd sleep with his head buried in her hair that he said he loved the smell of.

Mother and Papa never knew that David and Gretchen hadn't planned to live in America. They were looking at a small house in a nearby town when he was killed in an Army training accident. "I'll never see any action, I'm a quartermaster!" David would always say.

David never knew that they were going to have a baby. The celebratory candles were lit at the dinner table when the Army sent two soldiers to tell Gretchen that he'd been killed. The news was just too much for her and Baby, who left Gretchen only a few days after she buried her beloved David. Gretchen saw no need in making things worse, so she never told anyone and moved to Italy.

Now at twenty five, she was ready to go home. She'd been away from her family for far too long. Maybe they could forgive her for the choices she'd made. At least she could be close to them again. She missed her brothers and sisters and wondered if they had families of their own now. She prayed that they did; she wanted to go home. *I just don't know how to get out of this situation. I'm still a young woman and I'd like to start my life over, maybe even have a family of my own,* Gretchen thought as she made her way across the town square to the small cafe on the other side of the park.

"Guten abend," he said in perfect German.

"Abend," Gretchen replied as she tried to appear unmoved by this beautiful Negro man. He had the same complexion as David, with a muscular physique and perfectly straight white teeth.

"Sprechen Sie English?" he politely asked through his row of pearly whites.

"Ja. Yes I do," Gretchen said as she quickly transitioned to English, correcting herself.

"I'm new in town," he lied. "Is there a place to get an early dinner?"

"Yes, just around the corner, there," she said and she pointed in the direction of the nearby restaurant, feeling a certain nervousness that she could not explain.

"Thank you," he said as he stood displaying his height. Gretchen was a tall woman, but this handsome Negro man towered over her by at least a few inches.

"I was just on my way there," Gretchen unexpectedly discovered herself saying. Something about him moved her. Something more than the fact that he reminded her of the husband she'd lost so many years ago.

"Would you mind if I walked with you?" he asked.

"It's just around the corner," Gretchen said as she slowed her pace to allow him to walk beside her.

The restaurant was already serving its early dinner guests. There were only a few tables left, all reserved with the exception of one.

"You've been nice enough to show me this place. Would you like to join me?" he asked.

"I don't think I have any choice this evening," Gretchen said as she reluctantly accepted the chair he pulled out. She had become accustomed to taking her meals alone on her days off. But this man was so attractive and . . . *Boy, does he smell good.* He was wearing the same cologne that her husband had always worn.

As they shared the meal, exchanging small talk, Gretchen began to feel comfortable with this man. His personality was warm and he was very easy on the eyes. He seemed genuinely interested in her life and found her current work as a nanny for a teenage girl courageous.

"By the way, my name is Gretchen," she said as she thanked him for a nice dinner and stood to leave.

"It's starting to get dark. Please allow me to walk you home," he said.

Gretchen wondered if he would ask to see her again. At least she hoped that he would. She hadn't done anything even remotely resembling a date in a very long time. It was worth the stares that she received from acquaintances at the restaurant who were curious about this stranger she was dining with.

"So tell me a little more about the family you work for. You said the girl, Angel, is a typical teenager. Is she difficult? I would assume that she would be quite spoiled. Traveling around the world with her parents and a nanny."

"They are *not* her parents!" Gretchen responded abrasively without thinking. The word "parents" was definitely not a word she would use to describe Miss Emily Barker and Ricky. She found them both to be two of the most self-centered, self-absorbed people she had ever met. They had only one goal in life and that was to be together at all cost. Angel was paying dearly for that. Their sexual appetite was something for the history books. Gretchen had been sleeping with her pillow over her head for months now, just trying to drown out the daily sounds of their ecstasy. No need for an alarm clock with those two in the house! But this would have been inappropriate and too much information to share with a man she'd just met.

Gretchen wondered what the truth behind the lies was. If she knew the truth what would she do with it? How would it affect her employment? A job that she was really getting tired of. While she loved Angel with all of her heart, it was becoming apparent that there was a void in Angel's heart that she could not fill. Far too often, she witnessed Angel deep in thought. She seemed to be longing for something not obtainable in the fancy stores, restaurants or places they visited. Gretchen knew that she could no longer turn a blind eye to Angel's unhappiness and someday soon she would have to ask Angel the questions that would surely change everything for the both of them.

"They are friends of her parents who died a few years back," she said just as they reached the front entrance, telling the same lie that Miss Emily Barker had told so many times.

"Well, thank you for a lovely dinner," Gretchen added.

"You are very welcome. It is very nice to meet you, Gretchen. I think that Angel is very lucky to have you."

*

Gretchen sho is changing my ideas about what a real woman's like, no matter if she's big or small, Donnie thought. They were spending a lot of time together, and he felt bad about not sharing everything with her, especially since she was so open with him. He just couldn't do the same. There was too much at stake. Donnie had been secretly following them. Just waiting for the right time to rescue Angel. He knew that he would only have one chance and that there was no room for mistakes. If he messed this up, he was sure that they would take Angel somewhere where he couldn't follow. Donnie was in Europe illegally, and didn't have a valid passport. He saw the chance to sneak on the ship and took it. It didn't much matter what would happen to him if he couldn't get Angel back.

Now that Miss Emily was spending all of her time at the hospital, Angel and Gretchen were left alone. Donnie saved every penny he could make, eating scraps from the dining tables that he cleaned each night. He was even caught a few times and fired. But somehow, God was looking out for him, always replacing one job with another.

Gretchen wanted to return home to her family but she also loved Angel and didn't want to leave her with Miss Emily and Ricky. Angel was quickly becoming a woman and already looked like one. She needed Gretchen to look out for her. "No telling what she'll get herself into without me. Angel's smart," Gretchen would say. Angel was sometimes too smart for her own good; thinking that she knew a lot more than about the world than she actually did. Book smarts will only take you so far. Experience is always the best teacher and Angel hadn't experienced much.

Gretchen worried about "that devil", as she called Mr. Anderson. She saw the way he looked at Angel, as if he could rip her clothes off and ravage her right in front of everyone. Gretchen was sure that given the chance, he would take advantage of that sweet child. Angel would probably allow it, thinking it a confirmation that she was indeed a woman.

Donnie had never seen a person so relieved as Gretchen was when Mr. Anderson and Regina departed. Miss Emily was doing everything she could to make them stay, while Gretchen was screaming inside, "Get the hell out, *now!*"

He could not keep lying to her. They were sitting on a park bench in the town square across the street from the apartment when he decided to tell her. This could ruin his chances of ever getting Angel back, but he felt that he could trust his newfound friend. "There's something I've been wanting to tell you," Donnie said as Gretchen made circles in the dirt under her feet.

"Ja, we have become great friends."

"Gretchen, I haven't been honest with you. I've been following you all for quite some time. Angel is my daughter," he spurted out, not really knowing what her response would be.

"Well . . . I knew there was something wrong, but *never* expected this," she said, relieved.

"I am so sorry for misleading you. You've been a true friend to me, Gretchen."

"I knew those two weren't telling me the whole story. No way would parents treat their own child like they treat Angel. And money has little to do with it!"

"Gretchen, will you help me get my Angel back? I've never been there for her, but her momma loves her and needs her back. I am not even sure Angel will go with me willingly. I'll take her kicking and screaming if I have to."

"She might resist. But I know that she doesn't want to be here. I can see it in her eyes. She still calls out for her momma in her sleep. Miss Emily never answers. That's what made me question that whole arrangement. You have to act quickly. They're talking about going to another location where they can get better care for Ricky, maybe back to Germany. That would work for me because I would just leave once we arrived. If you take Angel, there'll be no reason for me to stay."

"God works in mysterious ways," Donnie said as he exhaled deeply, relieved to know that he'd made the right decision in confiding in Gretchen.

"I thought you were about to ask me to marry you!" Gretchen joked.

"Gretchen, if things were different, I just may have," Donnie said as he reached for her hand.

Gretchen wasn't anything like Sally, the only thing that they had in common was size. Sally was a *big* woman too. Difference was, Sally was *big* in all the wrong ways: *big* mouth, *big* attitude, with *big* no-count kids. Donnie married her during one of the lowest times in his life. He had been kicked out of the Army with a dishonorable discharge, with nowhere to go but back to Virginia and no Georgie. Her momma had lied to him. She told him that Georgie didn't want nothing to do with him. She told him that Georgie had taken a job in Baltimore like they planned but had decided to live her life without him.

God musta had his hand in it somehow, cuz when I think back on it, I shoulda known better. Shoulda been more sure of the love that woman, my Georgie, had for me.

I think the devil had his hand in it too. He knew my prideful thoughts. He used the one thing that truly mattered to me: my Georgie. He took her away and killed every dream I ever had along with it.

So I married Sally with her five boys. It wasn't all that bad at first. Sally seemed to really need me. I fixed up that ole shack of ours pretty well. The boys needed a daddy and I did the best that I could with them.

The oldest boy once went as far as to hit Donnie over the head with a cast iron frying pan that knocked him out cold for hours. They thought he was dead, so they threw him in a hole out back in the woods. When Donnie woke up, *he* thought he was dead. And still, his dumb ass went back to Sally. He didn't have nowhere else to go and she knew it.

Sally knew that he had never stopped loving Georgie. When Georgie showed up pregnant, everybody knew it was Donnie's baby she was carrying. Sally would talk down to him right in front of the boys. Then they started talking down to him too. Telling Donnie that he wasn't their daddy, even though he was the only daddy those boys had ever known. Sally and her boys treated Donnie like shit. They would wait until he'd had a few drinks, which he did often, and steal money right out of his pocket.

The worst times were when they happened to see Georgie and

Donnie's lil Angel. They'd see them around town from time to time. Hard not to, in a town as small as theirs. "You best not say shit to that bitch!" Sally would say as they approached them.

"Hello." Lil Angel smiled as Donnie ignored both her and Georgie, looking at the ground as they passed.

Sally sapped all the man right out of him. He didn't know why he stayed with her as long as he did. Guess he thought that they could help each other get over the pain they both bore for so long. It worked for a while. But there comes a time when each one of us has to do the work to get through our own pain. Sally wasn't willing to do the work. She wanted Donnie to stay right where she was—hurt and miserable. Guess it's true what they say, misery loves company.

Miss Emily made one grave mistake when she stole Donnie's lil Angel. She assumed that she could get away with it. She didn't know that Angel had a daddy who loved her. Donnie had been acting like a fool for long enough. The past didn't matter to him one bit. He wasn't there for Georgie and Angel all those years, but he was here now. He'd go to the ends of the earth for them. That's what he'd been doing for almost three years now. Everywhere Ricky and Miss Emily went, Donnie followed. He sneaked on the cargo ship bound for Germany, working on the farms there and in Italy; even cleaned toilets. Sometimes, he slept in barns or in alleys. Anything to be near Angel.

Now he had this one real chance to take Angel back home to her momma where she belonged and he was going to take it.

It's Time

It was a day just like any other day . . . *It's time*, he said, standing beside my bed like a dream. It had been such a long time since Charlie had visited me. *Get ready*, he said with his eyes before disappearing.

What was I supposed to do? *Get ready for what?* I thought as Gretchen knocked on my door.

"Morgen," Gretchen whispered. "It's time," she said, causing a chill to run down my back. "You must dress quickly," she said as she began removing my clothes from the dresser and placing them in my suitcase. *Not another trip!* I thought. You cannot take all of your things, but you will not need them."

"Where are we going?" I asked as I slipped into the jeans and the red plaid shirt she handed me.

"What's going on?" I asked as I slipped the still unopened envelope that Mr. Anderson had given me into my back pocket.

"You have to hurry," Gretchen said, ignoring my inquiry.

"What's for breakfast?" I asked.

"No time for breakfast this morning," Gretchen said as she handed me a thick slice of bread as we passed the kitchen. *Okay, now she's scaring me.*

"Hurry," she said as she picked up her bag at the front door and handed me mine; closing the door behind us.

There was a man waiting for us at the corner. As we drew closer to him, I was sure that I recognized him. But, it just couldn't be. But it was! My daddy! My daddy had come for me! I dropped my bag and collapsed in his arms.

"Hello Angel," he said—a voice that I had never heard. "I am here, child, to take you home to your momma," he said as I tightly held on to him.

"Miss Emily will return for lunch. We have to go now," Gretchen said as we ran to catch the next train going anywhere.

This time, there would be no note. No clothes stacked neatly on the bed. We were just gone.

The next train out of the station was bound to Frankfurt, Germany. I would be on the train for ten hours with this man people said was my daddy. Only a few moments ago, I heard his voice for the very first time. I still didn't know what he and Gretchen had planned. I wasn't sure that they knew either. But one thing was for sure, I would be far away from Miss Emily Barker and my momma's husband Ricky, and that was fine by me!

"That will be one hundred liras or fifty US dollars," the train attendant said. Both Gretchen and my daddy quickly responded by handing him $50. My daddy insisted that Gretchen allow him to pay and after about five minutes of negotiating with Gretchen, she allowed him to purchase our escape.

"It's the least I can do, Gretchen. You've taken such good care of Angel all of this time, keeping her safe."

"I love my Angel," Gretchen announced proudly, planting one of her momma-like hugs on me. This was the very first time that she'd ever said she loved me.

Once we settled in our cabin, Daddy asked me all the standard questions that grown folks ask.

"You sixteen now, right? How you doing in school? What grade you in?"

Our cabin wasn't as nice as the cabins that Miss Emily Barker insisted on when we traveled together, but that made no difference to me! I felt so happy to be away from her that I thought I might burst. I had no idea what was to become of me. This day was all that I had been dreaming of for almost three years and now that it was happening, it felt like a dream. A dream that I never wanted up wake up from.

Each time I'd sneak a look at my daddy, I discovered something new about him that I saw in myself. We had the same complexion, same pronounced forehead, and even the same perfectly straight white teeth. I couldn't stop smiling at him. Each time I did, he smiled right back.

"You okay, Angel?" Daddy asked.

"Yes sir. I'm just so happy. I could burst," I said through unexpected and uncontrollable tears.

"I'm so sorry that it took me so long to come get you," he apologized as he reached for my hand.

"It's okay, you're here now. I never expected you would be the one to rescue me. How's my momma?"

"Honestly, I don't know. I left shortly after you were . . . well."

"After Miss Emily took me," I said, completing his sentence.

"Well, yes."

"And how was Momma when you left?"

"Well, you know your momma loves you more than anything." *In pretty bad shape*, he thought. I could read his thoughts as if they were my own. I read his thoughts easier than I'd ever been able to read anybody's. His thoughts felt like mine. I don't know why, but they did.

After a multitude of stops, the train finally arrived in Frankfurt, Germany.

"This is where we say our goodbyes," Gretchen said as she stretched her arms out for me one last time.

"I thought you were coming with us. Frau Gretchen, you have to come with us!" I pleaded. In that one split second, my emotions plummeted from sheer joy to so much sadness that I couldn't contain it. Gretchen had protected me, cared for me, and loved me during the scariest time in my life. Now she was leaving. I didn't think it was possible to feel this much pain for anyone other than my momma. Why did it have to be this way? Would people continue to pop in and out of my life?

"No, Gretchen, please don't go. Daddy, please! Make her stay," I said, calling him Daddy for the first time.

"Angel, you must listen to me now. You are going to become a lovely young lady. I am sure that one day we will see each other again, but I cannot go with you now."

"No, no, no," I screamed, capturing the attention of every passenger departing the train as they witnessed me throw a temper tantrum like a five-year-old.

"Entschuldigen sie!" the German police officer said as he interrupted my temper tantrum.

"May I help you?" he asked.

"Nein, she is just a little upset," Gretchen answered nervously.

"Come here, child. What is your name? Why are you so upset? Are you okay? You can tell me," he said quietly. His questions seemed a little odd to me, even though I had been acting so foolishly.

"What is your name?" he repeated although this time it sound like a demand.

"My name is Angel," I quickly responded without thinking. As soon as the words came out of my mouth, I knew we were in trouble. And so did my Daddy as he exited our rail car and placed the last of our bags only a few feet from the policeman.

"You two will come with me," said the policeman sternly as he pointed at Gretchen and I.

"I don't understand," Gretchen said in German. "What's going on?" she said as she reached for my hand.

"Come with me," he repeated then, blowing his whistle, summoned additional officers who began pulling and tugging us in every direction.

"Hey! Take your hands of her!" my daddy said.

At that point, one of the officers who was by far the tallest, biggest man I had ever seen stepped between me, the other officers, and my daddy. He pushed my daddy away from us like a rag doll, causing him to fall to the ground. The other passengers who were departing the train began yelling and screaming as my daddy and the giant began their combative dance that seemed to only last for seconds, concluding in my daddy lying unconscious on the ground as Gretchen and I were hauled away.

"Daddy!" I screamed as several of the other officers grabbed each one of Daddy's arms and carried his unconscious body away.

"Daddy! Where are you taking my Daddy?" I screamed. I had met him only a few days ago and now they were taking him away.

"Angel stop! You're making things worse!" Gretchen pleaded. "Please think about what you're doing!" she said as she squeezed my arm.

"Come," the officer repeated as we followed him out of the station to his office that was located in the next block.

We had underestimated the lengths that Miss Emily Barker would go to have me returned to her. She had contacted every major train station for every route that departed our Italian town. She had everyone looking for us, informing them that Gretchen had kidnapped her daughter.

We might have gotten away if I hadn't acted like a spoiled child. Now we were being detained in two separate rooms where we were repeatedly asked the same questions for hours.

"Just tell the truth," Gretchen said as she was taken away. But did she really want me to tell the truth or was she just saying that for the police officer's benefit? If there was one time in my life where I really needed to read Gretchen's thoughts, it was now. And I got nothing.

Lucky for me, they never asked me anything specific. "What is your name? How old are you? Where do you live?" the policemen asked me.

"We will have to investigate this case to determine if what you say is true. Until then, do not try to leave Germany. Your father will be here shortly," the police officer said to Gretchen as they entered the empty room where I had been sitting for what seemed like hours. As soon they were gone, I began to cry.

As I looked into Gretchen's familiar face, all the fear that I'd been holding inside for the past few hours poured out of me. "Where's my daddy? Are we going to jail? Please don't let them send me back to Miss Emily Barker," I pleaded, clinging to Gretchen's waist for my life.

"This is now a case for the police. My father is on the town council and was able to talk them into releasing us to him."

"But . . . where is my daddy?"

*

Donnie woke up the small, sterile white German hospital room with a single chair beside the bed and a headache that felt as if his head were three times its size. It hurt just to open his eyes.

"Ja, das is good. You are awake," the nurse said as she quietly entered my room. He could hear her but he could not speak. The words were right there on the tip of his tongue, but he could not speak.

"Don't try to speak," she said. "You took a terrible blow to your head. Doctor will come talk to you soon."

Donnie tried to nod but he couldn't do that either. He felt the familiar feeling of his body floating above the bed. It was the same feeling he'd had during his last visit to a hospital after being beaten by the white soldiers who were supposed to be his Army buddies. They beat Donnie so badly that the Army doctors put him on morphine to ease the pain. Donnie hated it then and he hated it now. Here he was again, flying high on drugs that still could not totally mask the pain that consumed him. Donnie had no idea how long he'd been in the hospital, and more importantly, where his lil Angel was. The last thing that he remembered was being beaten and kicked by the German police as they literally threw him into a holding cell.

"Damn Americans, think they own the world. Well you're in our world now." They laughed as they kicked and beat him until he stopped fighting back. They beat him so badly, all he could do was curl up in a ball and take it until they stopped. Donnie had been running away from beatings from the white man his whole life. But this was a different kind of hate. It had nothing to do with color. These German police officers hated Donnie because he was an American, something no white man had ever called him. No matter where the Negro man go, seem like he always getting his ass wiped by somebody.

Donnie wanted to keep his eyes open but it just hurt too much. He was drifting in and out of consciousness. Each time he did, he found himself reliving the past; the good and the bad times. Seemed like the Lord was showing him all the things that he'd done in his life. Holding him accountable for it all. In one of his trips down memory lane, Donnie and Georgie were laying in the moonlight on the one and only night that they spent together. The feeling that he would never hold her in his arms again was breaking his heart over and over again. There was no amount of morphine that would ever ease that.

Then there were the memories of the sheer cruelty of Sally and her boys. "Please Lord, if you gonna take me, please let me see my lil Angel just one more time," Donnie prayed as he slipped out of consciousness once more.

"Donnie, can you hear me?" Gretchen asked, holding Donnie's hand as he struggled to figure out who she was. It had taken some time but with the help of her father, she was able to find him. The small hospital was only a few towns away from where her family lived. Donnie had been in the hospital for three weeks now. She had brought Angel to see him, but wanted to have a few minutes alone with him first. According to the way he felt, he knew that he was not getting any better. During one of his trips in and out of consciousness, he overheard the doctor say that every effort must be made to locate his family before it was too late. Donnie prayed that it was only a dream. But, by the look on Gretchen's face, he now knew that it was not.

"Angel is living with my family and me. They fell in love with her at first sight. She will be well cared for. Not to worry," Gretchen assured me as she sat beside by the bed. "You and she will be together soon," she lied as she pretended to look at the floor to wipe away her tears. "Would you like to see her? She's waiting right outside."

"Yes," Donnie indicated by blinking his eyes slowly as the pain traveled from his head to his shoulders, all the way down to the bottom of his feet. It was taking over now.

"Oh Daddy!" Angel said when she entered the room. "I am so sorry! This is all my fault!" Angel cried.

Donnie could not reach out to hold her as he so desperately wanted to. He couldn't even tell her how much he loved her. In desperation, he did what he had always done with his own momma after she passed away and would come to visit him as a child.

Angel, I hope that you can hear me. This is the only way that I can talk to you now. My momma had the gift and I just pray that you have it too.

"Oh Daddy! Yes, I hear you," Angel said.

My momma told me a long time ago that we came from good stock. This gift that you inherited from her will serve you well but only if you use it properly. Momma said this special gift was only for the girl children in the family. People didn't always understand it. Some even thought she was a witch, a Conga woman or something even worse. Can you see spirits too?

"Yes, Daddy. I'm so relieved to finally have someone that understands me. I've been keeping this secret for a very long time. I wondered why I could read your thoughts like my own and now I understand why," Angel said as they conversed in the all-white room.

Angel, don't be scared. I getting ready to go be with my momma now. I prayed that we would have more time together. But that just can't be. I want you to know that I love you with all my heart. I want you to know that no matter what people say, I love your momma. You might not understand it now, but she is the only woman that I ever loved. I was never happier than when I was with her. She's the finest woman I have ever known. I need you to do something for me.

"Yes, Daddy."

I need you to tell her that I'm sorry. I need you to tell her that I never stopped loving her. I need you to tell her that one day, we will be together in the moonlight once again and this time, I will never let her go, thought Donnie as he slipped away for the very last time.

"Daddy, Oh Daddy. I'll tell her, Daddy. I'll tell her, Daddy! I'll tell her, Daddy," Angel said as her voice became louder with each word. The doctor, the nurse and Gretchen were in the room now.

"I'm so sorry. He's gone," said the doctor.

Donnie was buried in the cemetery that Gretchen's family owned. The whole town came out to pay their respects. Donnie would have liked that.

Christmas Time—Hold On, Momma

During the Christmas season, Georgie could always feel the quiet excitement of the coming of the Lord. As a child, that excitement was more about the presents and seeing family that she hadn't seen since the last Christmas. This time, the only thing that she wanted for Christmas was to hold her lil Angel in her arms. Georgie wanted it so badly that her heart ached. It ached more than it ever had before. Not even the passing of her dear Sissy, her baby boy Charlie, or even her own momma had caused her this much pain. Georgie thought those things would kill her. *But dat ain't got nothing on the constant heartache and longing I feel to just see my child and hold her in my arms again*, she thought.

Georgie was holding on for dear life to Sissy's message sent in Regina's letter. Of all people, her hopes were now placed on a woman that she didn't even like. How could Georgie know that her momma's ole saying about never burning bridges would be the only thing that she would have to hold on to?

Georgie had to make it through Christmas. She had to pull herself together for Aunt Adele and Mr. Henderson who were coming for Christmas dinner. They had a nice dinner. But Georgie couldn't help but check the front window and door every so often. She was sure her lil Angel would be knocking on the door any minute. Dinner was finished, but still her lil Angel wasn't there.

"Well, I guess I better start heading back now. It's starting to snow again. I had a really nice time, Mrs. Evans. Thank you for inviting me," Mr. Henderson said as he started to put on his overcoat.

"What the hell? Yawl still calling each other Mr. Henderson and

Mrs. Evans?" Aunt Adele slurred after drinking too much of her own homemade wine. "Everything you two been through and you still acting like yawl not sweet on each other."

"Aunt Adele, stop," Georgie interrupted. Having a man was the last thing on her mind right now. It took all her strength just to make it through dinner. She would have been just fine with staying in her bed instead. No amount of pretending was going to work tonight. She missed her lil Angel too much.

"Like I said, I guess it's time for me to leave."

"Thank you for coming Mr.—" Georgie hesitated. "Okay, I'll walk with you to your truck. It's dark out there," she said, grabbing the oil lamp from the dinner table to lead the way.

"Aunt Adele can be so crazy sometimes," Georgie whispered as she and Mr. Henderson made their way down the path to his truck. Yeah, it was true that every once in a while she felt something for him but Georgie was not going to give in to that. No, not again. She was sure that her heart would just give out if . . .

"Crazy? She don't seem crazy to me. Maybe it's the wine giving me the nerve to say it, but you and I both know we likes each other and it's more than just as friends."

"I ain't been real good at picking a good man, ya know."

"Well, you ain't picking me. God chose you for me."

"And what if . . ."

"What if it don't work out?" he said, completing my sentence. "Then at least we can say that we tried. You ain't the only one scared here, ya know. Look at me with my one bad leg. I'm scared to death that you won't be able to see past this thing," he said, tapping on his leg. "But I care enough about you to take a chance. Can you?"

"It's been a long day. And maybe we done had too much to drink." This was all just too much for one day.

"My momma used to say a drunken man tells no lies."

Georgie nodded because her momma used to say the same thing. "Well, like I said, it's been a long day. Maybe we can talk about this later."

"Well, can we at least agree that we're friends and can start calling each other by our first name?"

"Yes, Charles, we can," she said, causing his eyes to light up.

"Merry Christmas, Georgie," he said.

Georgie could barely hear him as her mind began to wander, taking her to a place she hardly ever allowed it to go. Just for a moment she would allow her deepest desires to become real. The sound of Charles's voice was now being muffled by Georgie's imagination. A dream so real that she could hear the sound of footsteps on the gravel road and the thumping of her own heart.

Georgie and Charles had been standing out there on the path longer than she realized. The oil light was almost empty. It placed only a dim light on the three figures coming down the road toward them. She would not need light to make out who these people were.

"Oh my Lord, Charles, I think I sees . . ."

"Mommy, Mommy, I'm home!"

"Dear Lord, don't let this be a dream."

Her lil Angel was in her arms, holding Georgie tighter than she ever had. The other two figures belonged to Donnie and Regina. All three of them were covered with snow.

"I had a good idea where they might be, so I called an old Army buddy of mine."

"Right now, I don't even care. I got my lil Angel back. You're back where you belong," I said in between the kisses and hugs.

"What's going on out . . ." Aunt Adele began before seeing all of us standing in Momma's front yard. "Oh my Lord, my prayers done been answered. Hallelujah! Praise his name!" she said near the big tree where lil Charlie lay buried.

"This is the best Christmas since the coming of the Lord! Yawl come on in the house. There's still plenty of food left," I said, holding my lil Angel tightly and pushing Donnie and Regina down the path toward the house.

"Where you goin', Charles?" Georgie asked as he opened his car door. "Ain't no way this celebration gonna be complete without you. Come," Georgie said, taking his arm with her lil Angel by her side. "The Lord has truly blessed me this day."

If only this dream could come true. For just a second, she allowed herself to dream a powerful dream. Her lil Angel had been gone for years now. *Years, Lord! It's getting harder and harder for me to hold on to the dream that I'll ever see my child again,* Georgie thought as Mr. Henderson drove away.

Miss Emily had stopped sending her checks. Georgie didn't know how to take that. She tried with all her might to believe that Regina had found a way to steal her lil Angel back and was bringing her back to her. But she was afraid that it could mean something even worse. Maybe something had happened to her lil Angel. Maybe she'd tried to run away and was now hurt or worse. Charles knew that Georgie was no longer getting checks from the lawyer but was afraid to ask why. *Lord, please take care of my lil Angel. I don't care what happens to me, but please Lord keep her safe,* Georgie prayed.

Georgie just couldn't hold it in no longer. Dinner was over. Charles was gone. She couldn't hold back the tears as she looked at the Christmas tree filled with Angel's presents from all the years that she'd been away. Georgie didn't even know what she would like for Christmas any more. Miss Emily had taken all that from her. Years that she couldn't get back.

Angel isn't even little no more. She'll be sixteen years old now; practically a woman. Will I ever be able to see her again? Lord, I just can't do this no more. Just take me, Lord, take me, Georgie silently pleaded as Aunt Adele tried her best to comfort her. Georgie didn't have to explain to her what she was feeling. Aunt Adele knew. For years, she'd watched Georgie pretend that Angel was just away on a long trip. Aunt Adele knew about holding on to lies just to keep from going crazy. She'd been through the same thing with Sissy. *All dem years being laughed at and called all kinds of names made her understand my life in a way that not too many other people could. But tonight, even that isn't enough to ease my pain,* Georgie thought.

"Child, you gotta go on with your life. I know it's Christmas and we supposed to be all jolly and shit, but you's killin' yourself with all this heartache," said Aunt Adele, still feeling a little tipsy from the wine.

"If I don't hold on to dis dream, I'm gonna lose my mind for sho. I pray every night for my lil Angel. Don't know where she at, what dey doing to her, if she still miss me."

"Now child, you know she misses you. Dat child loves you to death. If she staying with dem, its cuz dey got her head all messed up. I knows she gonna come back. But you gotta go on with your life till she do. Just hold on, child."

Time To Go

The German police conducted a thorough investigation of my case and determined that they could no longer hold me. I suppose Gretchen's dad scared them into releasing me, threatening an investigation into how my daddy died.

There was no reason for me to stay in Germany now that Daddy was gone. Gretchen and her family treated me like family but I knew it was time to go home. We knew that Miss Emily Barker would not stop looking for us. Lucky for us, the letter of inquiry that she sent to the local police station was intercepted by Gretchen's dad who worked there.

"I think it's time for me to go home," I announced while having dinner with the family.

"You are welcome always in our home. You can stay here for as long as you like," Gretchen's dad said.

"Danke, Herr Schulz. I truly appreciate all that you and your family have done for me. I know my momma needs me and I need to go home."

"You will always have a home with us. You have brought Gretchen back to us and for that, we will always be grateful."

"So what now?" Gretchen asked as we cleared the last few dishes from the table. "I don't want you to go. After being away from my own family for so long, I understand why you must go but I'll miss you."

"And I'll miss you too. I'm just not sure how to get back home."

"I think I can help you with that, but you must do exactly as I say," Gretchen said in the familiar stern voice that I had heard so many times before and now loved.

Gretchen still had connections on the Army base in Frankfurt. She was able to convince the sergeant in charge of scheduling civilian flights to the United States that I was a military orphan. Gretchen told the sergeant that I'd become an orphan while traveling on holiday with my father who was a soldier. She'd glance over at me as I strategically sat outside the sergeant's office; hoping to capture some sympathy from the sergeant. If he accepted our request, I'd be able to travel home at no charge as the dependent of a deceased Army veteran.

Gretchen's plan worked. I would depart Germany at the end of the week. "Like Momma always said, God will make a way," I said after listening to Gretchen proudly describe her persuasive tactics to me.

"That is very true," Gretchen said as she retrieved a stack of mail from the post office in town on our way home. She shuffled through the mail, briefly stopped at one letter in the pile and then quickly placed all the letters in her purse. Once everyone had retired for the night, Gretchen opened the letter, dreading its contents. Gretchen had forgotten that she'd given Miss Emily Barker her parents' address when she applied for the nanny position.

Gretchen,

I hope that you receive this letter before you do any more damage to my family. Ricky is gone now and you have taken the one thing I have left. How could you be so heartless after all that I've done for you? I entrusted you with my most prized possession and you have stolen her from me. I don't know what you think you're doing but I will not allow you to steal my Angel. I will hunt you down to the ends of the earth and make sure that you rot in jail for the rest of your life.

Please send my Angel home.
Miss Emily Barker

Gretchen would have preferred to keep Angel with her. She didn't want to scare Angel, but she was reading about all the civil unrest happening in the States. The Negroes were resisting the discrimination that still enslaved them long after slavery was supposedly abolished. She didn't want Angel to be caught up in what was going on over there. But she also did not want to see her returned to Miss Emily Barker.

I've got to get Angel on that plane as soon as possible. Miss Emily could show up at our door at any time. I think she truly believes the lies that she's been living. Now that Ricky's gone, she will not stop. I just know it. Dear Lord, I know I haven't prayed to you in a very long time. I need you now. Please help me protect this poor child. She's been through so much. Please show me the way.

Momma, I'm Coming

Nervously, we stood in line at the bottom of the staircase of the huge C130 airplane. It wasn't like the planes I'd seen on television. This was the largest airplane that I had ever seen. Gretchen and I both know that we would lose out on our one chance we had of getting me out of Germany if anyone asked us to provide proof of my military dependency.

"Are you sure you really want to leave now?" Gretchen asked in between the hugs and kisses after the soldier waved us through the line.

"A part of me wants to stay and part of me wants to go," I said as the tears streamed down my face, stopping for my very last hug from Gretchen while the other passengers moved past us and climbed the staircase, some rudely bumping us.

"Angel, you know there is trouble in America for Negroes right now. Your life will not be as it was here. I am not sure this is the right thing to do. You could find yourself in the middle of civil rights problems and get hurt. You must be extremely careful. You are only sixteen! I don't think you should go alone," Gretchen said, panicking a little more with each word.

"I will be just fine . . ."

"You must write me as soon as you land in Dover, Delaware. Don't forget to ask the USO office to help you get the train home."

"Yes, I know." Although Gretchen was worried for me, this felt like an adventure to me. I wanted to do it by myself. I knew that I could do it. If there was one good thing that I learned while spending all those years with Miss Emily Barker, it was how to travel.

"I love you, Angel," Gretchen said, openly crying; something that I had never seen her do. "You have been the closest that I have come to having my own child. I will love you my whole life."

"And I love you too," I said as I carried my one bag up the tall, steep stairs, waved goodbye to Gretchen once more, and entered the plane.

I'm not sure what I expected the inside of the plane to look like, but this surely wasn't it! Colored people on one side of the plane and whites on the other. Women and children up front, although segregated in the same manner. My first mistake was to say hello to the young white lady and her child as I was directed to my seat. The other mistake I made was wearing my Dorothy Dandridge outfit on a plane full of young male soldiers. Just a few months ago, I would have been in heaven to have so much attention, now it made me feel uneasy. No need to read anyone's minds with regards to what these soldiers were all thinking. Their crude thoughts came in loud and clear as I passed them to reach my seat in the colored section, just in front of the pair of green curtains that separated passengers from freight.

It was going to be a long flight.

Most of the passengers were asleep when I was awoken by a familiar sound that immediately caused me to panic.

"Yes, yes, oh yes."

Just for a second, I thought that I was back in Italy with Miss Emily Barker and my momma's husband Ricky.

"Sssh! You gotta be quiet," the man's voice said from behind the curtain.

Through the space where the two curtains met, I had a clear view of a soldier and the young woman who had been so rude to me. He was standing in front of her facing me while she was sitting on top of the freight box with him between her legs, moving and pushing as her ponytail bobbed up and down. The more she screamed, the harder I found it to look away.

I had become familiar with the sounds they orchestrated but I had never actually seen two people together like this before. I nervously adjusted my seat as the soldier brushed the white lady's hair out of her face as her ponytail fell apart. Now, he was looking directly at me.

You like this huh? You wanna join us? he thought as he increased his thrusting movements, keeping his eyes affixed on me. *You are the most beautiful girl I have ever seen!*

"Uh, uh, yes, yes, yes . . ." she climactically screamed. And then it was over.

The young soldier zipped up his pants and returned to his seat while the lady pulled up her stockings and panties and returned to her sleeping child as if nothing more than a handshake had occurred.

Was this all that I had to look forward to? There had to be more to love than this. I would never allow myself to be used like that. I couldn't understand why Momma would spend her entire life praying for something as crude as this . . . I didn't understand it at all.

The plane landed at the Dover Air Force base in Delaware at 04:00 the next morning. We were escorted to the military customs office for processing. I had no idea what I was supposed to do so I just followed everyone else.

"Passport and orders please," the white soldier behind the podium quietly repeated as each person progressed in line.

When it was my turn, I handed him my passport that Gretchen had stolen out of Miss Emily Barker's desk drawer and the papers that the sergeant in Germany had given her.

"Orders please," he quietly asked again.

"This is all that I have."

"What do you mean, this is all you have!" he barked. "*Fuckin' niggers . . .*"

"I am an orphan and . . ." I said, trying to hold back the tears and quiet my heart that was thumping in my chest; I hadn't expected him to yell at me. Would they make me return to Germany? Or even worse, Italy!

"I don't care nothing 'bout that. Either you have your orders or you don't!" he barked again, this time standing.

"Hold on now, Private!" said the Negro soldier standing in the line next to me. "I'm sure we can figure this out without all that."

"Yes, sir," said the white soldier.

"Ma'am, I'm gonna need to you to come with me, okay?" the handsome young Negro soldier said. No one had ever called me ma'am before. I liked it.

We must have gone to every office he could think of. Somehow, Lieutenant Antoine Deco was able to secure me a seat on the military bus headed south.

"Ma'am, the bus will depart here at thirteen hundred hours. That's one o'clock today. You can wait here at the USO until then. They have food and drinks available. You'll have no more problems from anyone. I can promise you that," he said as he placed my bag on the seat next to me in the waiting area.

There was something about his accent that just felt romantic to me. He seemed to sing instead of talk, even when he gave orders to the soldiers. The snares and stares didn't seem to bother him one bit. He seemed confident in his position, walking with a prideful gait that I had never seen any other Negro man exhibit.

"Thank you so much for all of your help. I would probably still be trying to explain my situation if it weren't for you."

"Glad I could be of help, ma'am," he said as he shook my hand and quickly exited the building.

I spent the rest of the morning pretending to watch the TV with bad reception in the smoke-filled area that was segregated by a knee wall as children on both sides of it had their diapers changed, screaming and hollering, as their mothers pretended not to see me; Negro and whites alike. Gretchen was right, I would have to become accustomed to living in the United States all over again.

"Bus leaves in fifteen minutes!" the bus driver finally announced. The bus had two doors, a front door for the whites and a middle door for the colored to gain access to the back of the bus. When I was a kid, Momma had told me stories about her trip to Baltimore. It was sixteen years later and things were still the same. I was on my way to be with Momma again after all these years, but still this separation bothered me. It was just wrong. It was so American. I planned to spend the next ten hours just gazing out the window. Just the thought that Momma and I would be together brought tears to my eyes.

"Is this seat taken, ma'am?" He smiled.

"Well no. I didn't know . . . well." All of a sudden I couldn't speak. I was too excited about spending the next ten hours with Lieutenant Antoine Deco.

New Beginnings

Lieutenant Antoine Deco was like no other colored man that I had ever met. He was so proud of his heritage. He said he was Creole from the French speaking part of Louisiana. His people had a little bit of everything in them, just like a big ole pot of gumbo: African, Spanish, Indian, Irish, German and probably some others too, he said. There was something about him that felt so comfortable. Maybe it was the melody in his words, the smell of his intoxicating cologne, or maybe it was the fact that he treated me like a lady. He treated me like someone that he could be romantically interested in, and considered a potential soul mate.

I intentionally disallowed myself to eavesdrop on his thoughts as we shared our bus ride speaking of generalities. It just felt wrong and very unnecessary to listen to his thoughts. Although I was able to tune out his thoughts, there was just no way to tune out the lewd comments made by the other soldiers accompanying us on our journey "down south".

"Woo wee, that dress is fitting her like a glove in all the right places. So tight, look like someone painted it on her. I could do some real damage with this one," the balding solider said as he allowed me to pass in order to reach my seat.

Um, um, um, thought another.

Based on the things these men thought, it would seem as though I passed them wearing no clothes at all!

I am confident that my bus ride would have been miserable without Lieutenant Deco. Gretchen was right. Just because I had the figure to pull off a Dorothy Dandridge dress did not mean that I should wear one, especially around so many soldiers who were more than eager to accommodate me with what the dress implied.

Lieutenant Deco seemed genuine with very little to hide. I, on the other hand, was evasive with him, not forthcoming about anything that would really matter, like the fact that I was allowing him to flirt with me in the most respectful way, while I failed to mention that I was only sixteen years old.

"My apologies, ma'am," said Lieutenant Deco. "Some of us haven't seen a single colored woman as lovely as you since we left the US."

He thinks I'm lovely, I thought.

"It's okay. I have to be honest, I haven't seen this many colored people in one place, period!" I said, leading us both to break out in laughter.

He had dimples that seemed to appear only when he laughed. What a beautiful man he was. I never thought that a man could be beautiful but he was in every way.

He told me to call him Deco. That's what all of his friends back home called him because he was the last male survivor in his family. With all that pride running through his bloodline, the other Negro men in his family were either found, "hanged by the side of the road or dead from being worked to death." His momma would warn him about that prideful nature whenever he stepped foot out of the house.

He had a thin build, tall and lean. With just a little work, he probably could have passed for white but Deco said he was all Negro and proud of it. He had light brown eyes and hair that was cut close around the sides and waved perfectly to one side on top to fit under his hat. Aunt Adele would have definitely called him pretty and she would have been right. He told me that as he got older, he quickly discovered that like so many other males in his family, he would not survive if he remained in his little hometown of five hundred people. It was a town where colored people were still treated just a tad better than slaves by the older residents. Most of the older white men were still calling black men, "boy". A colored man had to be careful of his every step. Any mistake could land him in jail or worse. It was just too much to take for a man with as much pride as the Deco men had.

The younger generation were trying to change things. Even the young white men caught hell for trying to change things. At best, they were called nigger lovers. Some found themselves receiving the same treatment as we did.

"In some ways, I think that it's best that we colored people stayed separate from the whites," Deco said just above a whisper as we huddled next to each other, speaking of things that should not be overheard.

"Why do you say that?" I asked, trying not to look in his eyes too long for fear he'd see how captivated I was by him.

"Growing up in that small town, I saw a lot of things that were just not right. Blacks beating up white boys for looking at their girls. The good ole boys stringing up young black boys for the lies that white girls told. It's just too hard to live together."

"My granddaddy passed for a long time, until he fell in love with grandma who was as black as the night. She'd come into his store every day to buys fresh eggs for the house she worked in. He would always say that he'd never seen anyone as black or as beautiful as she was. At first, she wouldn't even talk to him, cuz she thought he was a white man. It wasn't like he ever said he was white, folks just assumed that he was and he allowed them to think it.

"Granddaddy was smart. He was planning for our future. He saved every penny that he could so that his children and his, 'children's children could go the college'. That's what he would always say as we sat around the table having Sunday dinner.

"When Momma died shortly after giving birth to my sister Delphinine, my grandparents took us in. He made sure that I finished high school. When I told him that I didn't want to go to college, he was real upset with me. I was at the top of my class, even if it was just a little school for colored children. He pushed me to apply to the West Point Military Academy, knowing that my chances for acceptance were pretty slim. West Point had a long history of doing whatever was necessary to keep Negroes out. But I got in.

"That's not to say that it was easy. I had to leave my family to attend the academy in New York. I had classmates who wouldn't speak to me, refused to shower in my presence or even sit at the same table with me during meals. Still, it was all worth it. It was a happy day for my family when I graduated from the academy at the top of my class.

"After experiencing all of that and still not getting the respect from my soldiers because I'm colored, makes me wonder if it's all worth it. I'm tired of having to demand the respect that the white man receives so freely. I'm tired of fighting for every little thing I get and then having to defend my right to have it.

"But, that's enough about me. Plus, this conversation is getting a little heavy. Tell me about yourself. What were you doing in Germany? Were you studying abroad?"

"Yes, my adopted parents wanted me to experience something different from what was going on here in the United States," I lied. "I've been away for about three years now." I wasn't ready to share everything with him. "Things are changing here. I can only hope that it's for the better."

"So how old are you? If you don't mind me asking," he said directly, causing my heart to pound.

"I'll be eighteen in a few . . ."

"Whew! I'm so glad to hear you say that!" he interrupted. "You look a little younger but I can't imagine your parents would allow you to travel alone like this if you were younger. I'll be twenty two later this month. I haven't spent my birthday with my family in almost four years, so I thought I'd surprise them."

"That's so nice. Yes, I'm sure that they'll be happy to have you home again." I said, relieved that we were changing the subject.

"Next stop Richmond, Virginia!" yelled the bus driver.

"Well dear, this is where we part, I guess."

It was going to take some time before anyone could call me dear and not make me cringe. "It was very nice to meet you too, Deco."

"My daddy always told me that one day I would meet a nice girl. I think I just met her," he said. *I think I just found my angel*, he thought as he held my hand for a split second before he stepped off the bus by way of the side door, followed by all the other soldiers.

If he had to leave me, then I'm happy to see him taking those knuckleheads with him, I thought, using a new word Deco taught me.

For the next few hours, I tried to figure out what I would say to my momma. How could I explain away all the pain I caused her? After going over it in my head again and again, I decided to just tell her everything, but not all at once. How could anyone survive my story and have it topped off with the news that the love of her life, my daddy, was now gone?

One thing was for sure, I was going to change out of this ridiculous outfit before I saw my momma!

Although Momma thought she hated Daddy, I knew that deep inside of her hatred was love and an intense hurt caused by the promises that Daddy had taken with him when he left to join the Army. Too often, people take love for granted as if it's something that will keep when put on a shelf. Love is like anything else held dear. It has to be nurtured and cared for. Life's circumstances come into play far too often that can destroy even the most sincere heart, leaving nothing but despair and longing in its place.

I would try my best to live a life without making so many mistakes. I'd experienced so much in the last three years. Miss Emily Barker had taken me all over the world only to teach me that all I needed, all most people wanted, was love. Momma wanted it. Miss Emily Barker wanted it. My momma's husband Ricky wanted it, as well as so many people that I had met along my journey.

The bus dropped me off about five miles outside the town of Baxter, Virginia, just one town over from my momma's house. I had been traveling for days now with only the excitement of seeing my momma powering me. It would be dark once more in an hour or so. Only after walking several miles did anything begin to look familiar. The first thing that I noticed was our church. As I got closer, I could see that all the windows in our beautiful church were broken. There was a cross on the lawn. At first, I thought that maybe the congregation had organized a special winter ceremony as they sometimes did, but the closer I came to the church, the more obvious it became that this was not the work of the congregation.

The charred upside down cross positioned at the end of the church driveway said all that needed to be said. It served as an obvious representation of the struggle going on between the colored and the whites in our little town and across the United States.

The church was less than a mile or so from Mr. Henderson's store. I could see the light shining in his back room window like a beacon of safety. I had to get off this road. With so much turmoil going on, it just was not safe. No one was expecting me. No one would ever know what happened to me if the people who put the cross up decided to return tonight. Maybe I should pick up the pace a little. I was once again happy that I had changed into my sensible clothes: jeans, a simple white shirt and sneakers. My only mistake was wearing such a light-colored shirt. I didn't want anyone to see me as I made my way to Mr. Henderson's store. It was dark now. There were very few street lights but I had no choice. Momma's house was still a few miles away. I didn't want to push my luck by trying to make it there in the dark.

"Who's there?" Mr. Henderson yelled as I pounded hard on his store front door.

"It's me, Mr. Henderson. Miss Georgie's daughter, Angel," I yelled as I took a step back from the door. I didn't want to get shot. With everything that was going on, this was a real possibility.

"Angel, is that really you, child?"

"Yes sir."

"Good Lord, child! Your momma been going crazy waiting for you to return home," he said as he placed his baseball bat by the door and slowly opened it.

"Yes sir."

"There's a lot going on right now. One can't be too careful," he said, answering my silent inquiry about the bat.

"Yes sir."

"You alright, child?"

"I will be as soon as I see my momma. Can you take me to her, Mr. Henderson?"

"It is too dangerous for us to go out on the road tonight. We'll be on our way as soon as there's enough daylight in a few hours. Until then, you're welcome to rest here."

"I'm sorry, Mr. Henderson. I don't mean to be a bother. I just didn't know where to go after I saw what was done to our church.

Then I saw your light on and . . ."

"I'm glad you came here. Funny thing is, I almost never keep my lights on for very long. God musta meant for you to make your way here," he interrupted. "Your momma is gonna jump for joy when she sees you," he said as he handed me a blanket and a pillow for the small cot that he placed near the wood stove for me where he had shared so many treasured moments with my momma.

"Thank you so much for this."

"No need to thank me. I'm happy to help."

It Ain't Over Yet

The day started just like any other day with the sun coming up and showering us with light. Mr. Henderson and I quickly hopped in his truck to make our way to Momma's house. The closer we got to Momma's house, the harder my overly excited heart pounded in my chest. As we drove along the now paved road, nothing looked the same to me anymore. Momma had done such a nice job fixing up the house. I don't think that I would have recognized our home if it weren't for Mr. Henderson pointing it out to me. Our home now sat among several other houses that were built on the adjoining lots. There were so many cars in the driveway.

"Well, that's strange," said Mr. Henderson. "I ain't never seen this many cars on this road before."

That's when I saw Momma come out our front door accompanied by two white men, holding her arms. I was immediately taken back to the sight of my daddy being beaten and taken away by the German policemen. I jumped out of the truck before Mr. Henderson could come to a complete stop, forgetting my manners, without even saying thank you.

They were taking my momma out of the house in bare feet, still wearing her nightgown, with rollers in her hair. She did not resist. She knew better than that. I could hear her praying the whole time. This was the very last straw for her.

Lord, it don't matter no mo. You done took my child. She ain't never coming back. It don't matter what dey do to me, she thought.

By the time I reached the driveway, the policemen had already pulled away.

"Momma, I'm here," I yelled although I knew she couldn't see me. "Where are they taking my momma? No dear Lord, not again!" I screamed, panicking at the sheer thought of living through yet another loss. This just could not be. *Dear Lord, please don't take my momma. I've come so far. Please Lord*, I prayed as I fell to my knees in my momma's front yard.

"Come, child," Mr. Henderson said as he unsuccessfully attempted to comfort me. "Those police are local. We need to follow them and find out what's going on."

We sat in the small waiting room at the police station for most of the day. No one would answer our questions about where Momma was being held or why they were holding her. We were afraid to push the issue for fear of what they might do to Momma, and to us for that matter.

"Georgie is in a lot of trouble," said Mr. Benton. He'd known my momma since she was a young woman taking in his parents' laundry. "I just can't believe she done what they're accusing her of. Something just ain't right."

Momma was being charged with child abandonment and intent to fraud. Miss Emily Barker was accusing Momma of selling me to her and trying to steal me back. She even had a list of payments made to Momma for the purchase. The police were not believing Momma's side of the story.

"Why would a woman like Miss Emily Barker steal your child? She could very easily adopt a child if she wanted to," the police inquired. "Because she's sleeping with my husband and they want to have a black child," was the answer but not one that would help Momma's case. The police had no report of my kidnapping on file. Momma never reported it to them. This did not help our case. So after hours of interrogation, Momma just stopped answering their questions.

"We are holding your mother indefinitely, until we can get to the bottom of this. I'm sorry," said Mr. Benton. "I'm afraid that you are going to need a lawyer . . ."

"Sir, can we see her?"

"I'm afraid not. She has not been cooperative and therefore no visitors are permitted. We'll be moving her to the Smithfield Psychiatric Center tomorrow for evaluation. Again, I'm truly sorry but there's nothing that I can do."

Mr. Henderson and I quickly departed the station after thanking Mr. Benton for his help. I mustered up enough strength to walk out of that police station without collapsing. I would not give these policemen the satisfaction of witnessing my pain.

It took us another three weeks before we were able to locate where the police had taken Momma. She had stopped eating all together by then and was now being force-fed and heavily medicated. Finally we were able to see her.

"Momma, it's me!" I whispered to a non-responsive woman who only lightly resembled my momma. Her hair looked as if it hadn't been combed in days and she was in dire need of a good scrubbing. Mr. Henderson and I had asked everyone who would listen to us to consider taking our case. No one would. "You would just be giving away your money. You don't have a case. You will never be able to prove your mother's innocence."

As I sat in the visiting room, holding my momma's hand, I knew that we needed to get her out of here as soon as possible. The light was fading from Momma's eyes. Her spirit had been broken.

"I know Donnie gone. He come visiting last night," Momma announced.

"Oh, Momma. I'm so sorry."

"Ricky, he gone too. We all been walking round in the wilderness for year now. Following dat devil, Emily Barker. She gonna git what's comin' to her. You just wait and see. You just wait and see. You just wait and see. You just wait and see. You just wait and see," she hysterically repeated over and over again until the attendant ended our visit and escorted her out of the visiting area.

"We must do something quickly. Momma's losing her mind in that place," I confessed to Mr. Henderson on our drive back to Momma's house. He didn't respond at all. What more was there to say? Miss Emily Barker was winning.

"I'll pick you up same time tomorrow," Mr. Henderson said.

"Yes sir," I said as I exited his truck and waited for him to drive off before making my way to Miss Emily Barker's house. I knew she was there. Charlie warned me of her arrival just two nights prior. At the time, I wasn't sure what I was supposed to do about it, until now.

Miss Emily Barker was standing on her front porch waving at me as if I were a long awaited guest. "I knew you would come. I'm so happy that you were able to get away, dear," she said as she greeted me with a hug.

"Yes ma'am." I was going to have to play along with her if my momma had any chance of being released.

"Miss Emily, what have you done? You know my momma didn't steal me back. Don't you remember telling Gretchen to send me ahead of you, so that you could take care of Ricky? I was so sorry to hear of his passing," I lied.

"I don't recall that, dear. So much has happened I don't know what's real and what's not anymore." *I'm so glad that you're here. I thought you'd never come back,* she thought, verifying that I was doing the right thing.

"I can't live in my momma's little shack. I belong here with you. But people will talk if we don't get her out of that place. We have to find a way to get her out of that place so that we can be together."

"You want to stay with me?" she asked as she tried to reconcile the words.

"Of course! Why wouldn't I? You've been so good to me. Plus, you're my family now. How could I ever go back to living like that? But we have to get Momma out of there first."

"Yes, we can go away again. I can call my lawyers in Baltimore and have them explain the whole thing. Your momma will be released immediately."

With one short phone call, Miss Emily Barker erased the cloud hanging over my momma's head and she was released to Aunt Adele the very next day. I was standing on Momma's front porch when she, Aunt Adele and Mr. Henderson arrived.

"If that bitch think she gonna git away with this she got another think comin'. I'm so tired of white folk just doing whatever they feel like to us," said Aunt Adele as she carefully helped Momma into her house. Mr. Henderson said that Momma had not spoken a single word during the trip home. Aunt Adele, on the other hand, had been cussing and shouting the entire way.

"How do we know Miss Emily won't try something else?" Mr. Henderson asked.

"We don't," I admitted. "But for now, we have Momma home where she can rest." I sat next to my momma holding her hand. "I'll stay with Miss Emily until we can find a way to fix this thing once and for all."

"No!" Momma screeched, sounding like a cat in pain as she held onto to me for dear life. "Don't go! Something bad 'bout to happen. Pleeease, don't go."

"Momma, don't worry. I'll be fine. I'll be back early tomorrow morning, I promise."

"Don't know why we tip-toeing around that bitch. She should be the one in jail. I ain't kissing her ass," Aunt Adele continued.

"Aunt Adele, we gotta be smart about this. Smarter than Miss Emily."

"She need her ass kicked. That's what she need."

"That won't solve our problem. Promise me that you'll let me try to fix this. Take care of Momma and I'll be back in the morning," I said as Mr. Henderson took my bag to his truck with Momma repeating the same lines over and over, "Don't go. Don't go. Don't go. Don't go."

All Things Work for Good

For more than a month now, I spent all my nights at Miss Emily Barker's house in the guest bedroom down the hall from her. She was keeping a close eye on me, ever since I had returned to live with her as promised. She only allowed me to leave the house to go to visit my momma for an hour and to go to church. She insisted that her driver take me anywhere that I wanted to go. I knew this was her way of controlling me. Each time that I returned, she'd hug me like her life depended on it.

"I'm so glad to see you. How was your day?" *I thought you might not come back.*

Miss Emily hired a cook and housekeeper and paid them enough money to overlook her rude and now somewhat strange behavior. "Come dear, it's time to eat," she called to me.

"Don't forget to change the sheets on my bed every day. Ricky doesn't like dirty sheets," she'd instruct them, knowing full well that Ricky had passed away months ago. She refused to believe that he was gone, interrupting me whenever I approached the subject with her.

"I'm making plans for our next adventure, Angel dear," she announced as we sat quietly at opposite ends of the table in her formal dining room. The large room could easily accommodate forty people, but made it extremely difficult to have a conversation with her, as she intended. *It's time to get out of this backwards town.* "As soon as Ricky arrives, we'll be leaving. Just like when we were in Germany."

"Yes ma'am." I had to find a way to get away from her.

"Lord, please help me find a way to get out of here," I prayed, falling asleep in my tears as I had done so many night since moving into Miss Emily's house.

Not to worry. This will all be over very soon, Charlie said as he stood beside my bed with two figures behind him that I couldn't make out.

"Please don't go. Please don't leave me alone with her," I pleaded.

You are never alone, Charlie said before vanishing.

"Yes, yes, yes my love!" I heard Miss Emily coo from her bedroom as I silently passed to use the bathroom. "I will prepare everything for you," she said in her sleep. Miss Emily was losing her mind for sure.

I returned to my room with a new sense of confidence. Charlie had not forgotten me. He had never failed me before. If he said this would be over soon, I was sure that it would be. And I would be ready, I thought as I fell into sleep. Charlie visited me every night for the next seven nights. Each time repeating the same message. *This will all be over soon.*

It was a night just like all the other nights. *Time to go,* Charlie said, but this time Aunt Sissy and my daddy were with him. All three of them were covered in light similar to the light around a candle, bright around their figures and dimming outwardly. Although I wasn't sure if I were dreaming, I didn't ask any questions. I simply grabbed the bag that I had prepared and stuffed under my bed and followed them down the stairs. Their light was so bright, I couldn't see anything else except for it. There was no need to turn on any lights in the house as we made our way down the stairs.

We exited the house into pitch black darkness and began making our way down the path to the front gate as I had done so many times before. That's when I heard Miss Emily Barker calling out to Ricky from her bedroom window. "I knew you'd come back to me, my love! We will make love by candlelight tonight, my love."

The further we moved down the path, the brighter the light from her room became. Then I saw that it wasn't light at all, but fire with

Miss Emily Barker standing within it. "Oh Ricky, I can't live without you. I can't be in this world without you!" she screamed as the fire consumed her. *God forgive me for the things that I've done,* she thought.

The driver, housemaid and cook were running around, frantically trying to put the fire out until they were forced to leave the house and save themselves, joining me on the front lawn under the big tree. I turned to thank Charlie, Aunt Sissy and my daddy but they were gone. *Thank you for saving me and making things right,* I thought.

The sun was rising now. Bringing with it a new beginning. This day would not be just another day. It would be the first day of the rest of my life. I would use it and everyone hereafter wisely.

THE END . . .

Reviews

If you enjoyed *Tethered Angel,* please consider leaving a rating and review on Amazon and Goodreads

Reviews and feedback are important to an author, as well as other potential readers, and would be very much appreciated. Thank you.

**You can connect with Author T. M. Brown
through her social networks and author's website.
She is always happy to hear from her readers:**

Facebook
https://www.facebook.com/pages/Author-TM-
Brown/135539973292576?ref=hl#!/tina.brown.92754397

Twitter
https://twitter.com/TbrownM

Author's Website
http://www.author-tmbrown-com.